High stakes

"Despite your protestations, it's quite a serious consideration with you now. Us sleeping together," he added for absolute clarification. "But being you, a first-class fighter—" his lips twisted "—there are certain inherent difficulties about laying down your arms."

"I haven't laid down any arms because I don't want to. If you really believe I'm in a hurry to add myself to the long list of women you've been intimate with, you're—"

She stopped abruptly as he got up, picked up the towel and laid it over a chair, then came toward her.

"I would disagree about it being such a long list, but you know, Jane, there are some women who never know how to lay down their arms, and it's often partly because they have this secret desire to wrap them tightly around someone. Is that your problem? I'd be quite happy to be that someone, assuming you could be honest about it."

LINDSAY ARMSTRONG married an accountant from New Zealand and settled down—if you can call it that—in Australia. A coast-to-coast camping trip later, they moved to a six-hundred-acre mixed-grain property, which they eventually abandoned to the mice and leeches and blackflies. Then, after a winning career at the track with an untried trotter, purchased "mainly because he had blue eyes," they opted for a more conventional family life with their five children in Brisbane, where Lindsay now writes.

Books by Lindsay Armstrong

HARLEQUIN PRESENTS
1327—A LOVE AFFAIR
1439—THE DIRECTOR'S WIFE
1487—LEAVE LOVE ALONE
1546—A DANGEROUS LOVER
1569—DARK CAPTOR
1593—AN UNUSUAL AFFAIR

HARLEQUIN ROMANCE
2582—PERHAPS LOVE
2653—DON'T CALL IT LOVE
2785—SOME SAY LOVE
2876—THE HEART OF THE MATTER
2893—WHEN THE NIGHT GROWS COLD
3013—THE MARRYING GAME

Don't miss any of our special offers. Write to us at the following address for information on our newest releases.

Harlequin Reader Service
P.O. Box 1397, Buffalo, NY 14240
Canadian address: P.O. Box 603,
Fort Erie, Ont. L2A 5X3

LINDSAY ARMSTRONG

The Seduction Stakes

Harlequin Books

TORONTO • NEW YORK • LONDON
AMSTERDAM • PARIS • SYDNEY • HAMBURG
STOCKHOLM • ATHENS • TOKYO • MILAN
MADRID • WARSAW • BUDAPEST • AUCKLAND

ISBN 0-373-11626-8

THE SEDUCTION STAKES

Copyright © 1992 by Lindsay Armstrong.

CHAPTER ONE

JANE MATHIESON ran up her driveway with her heart pounding and as if pursued by a variety of demons.

In fact there were two. Youngish louts who must have been lurking behind the bus shelter as she'd alighted and started to walk the two blocks home through the chill late evening.

She hadn't noticed them for about half a block, mainly because she'd been wearily reviewing a disastrous day that had begun with her car refusing to start, a day that had continued through one crisis after another at work and ended, or so she'd thought, with her having to take a bus home because of a positive dearth of taxis. Then she'd suddenly heard the two sets of footsteps behind her, keeping pace with a chilling sort of uniformity, and she'd glanced round and, without having to use much intuition, realised she had a problem.

Keep your head, she'd advised herself. You're supposed to be good at that anyway, and they might just be testing you out.

Whether they were she was destined not to know, because as they started to make increasingly obscene comments her nerve broke and she took to her heels.

All the same, as she sprinted round the corner of the house, not only was her heart pounding with fear but she had to stop and double up with a stitch. But as she tried to control her breathing and at the same time pick up every little sound she heard faint, sneering laughter

5

then a car door banging further down the road and its engine roaring to life. It drove away at speed.

She let out a long quivering breath, straightened and reached into her pocket for her keys. They weren't there. She sat down on the back step and started to fumble through her bag but even as she did she had a very clear mental picture of her key-ring, which held the house keys as well as her car keys, lying on the kitchen table where she'd tossed it that morning in a fit of frustration.

She swore beneath her breath and tried to remember which window she might have left ajar—her bedroom, she decided—and how she was going to reach it. The house was a typical Queensland old colonial—in other words, set up on stilts.

By the time she did reach the window by way of a precarious selection of boxes and barrels, she was panting and sweating, she'd laddered her tights, torn a hole in her skirt and broken a nail, and she all but fell through it, landing on her feet but only just, and what followed made everything else that had happened to her since she'd stepped off the bus pale into significance.

Because, with a blood-curdling roar very reminiscent of a Maori *haka*, a huge form rose up from her bed, and, even trailing sheet and blankets, tackled her about the knees with unerring aim and felled her to the floor.

Jane had never screamed in her life before, had actually wondered how it was done, and was to realise it was a quite spontaneous reaction that was probably impossible to simulate—and that it was in fact an extremely useful weapon, especially when you didn't seem to be able to stop.

It certainly caused the monster attacking her to go still, to utter a very human expletive in tones of also very human surprise, and to begin to attempt to disentangle them from each other.

But despite these signs of humanity Jane found herself still panic-stricken, and she kicked and clawed with all the strength she had left.

'Hang on, ma'am,' the monster said with evidence of exertion in *his* voice as well as some hateful amusement, 'I think we might be at cross-purposes . . .'

But Jane redoubled her efforts despite this advice, causing her protagonist to swear again and then to say very firmly, 'That's *enough*, lady. Look, I don't want to hurt you but . . .' And, so saying, he took both her wrists in one large hand, placed his other hand over her mouth, and, deftly kicking aside a blanket, pinioned her knees together between his own.

At last Jane's adrenalin gave out, her eyes dilated, and with a sob of fear she went limp.

'Now don't faint on me,' the voice above her warned. 'I'm going to pick you up and put you on the bed,' it added, and continued, 'where I was having a peaceful, righteous, well-deserved sleep until you broke through the window, causing me to wake and believe I was being burgled. I'm going to take my hand away now, but if you start screaming again I'll have to put it back—I have absolutely no designs on your virtue or otherwise. Ready?'

The hand was removed and Jane took a gulp of air but didn't scream.

'Good—we're making progress. Here we go.' The voice was patient and amused again but the hands that lifted her were both strong yet gentle as she was laid on the bed, and finally the bedside lamp clicked on.

Jane blinked as the soft light dispelled the darkness— and dispelled her monster theories. For although the man sitting on the edge of the bed beside her was built along rather grand lines, he was also one of the best-looking men she'd ever seen—but not only that; he had an undeniably peacable air about him. Was it those sleepy blue eyes? she wondered. Or the thick dark hair or, as it curved his lips, a particularly humorous smile that made you want to respond?

She shut her mouth with a click then opened it almost immediately. 'This is my bed!'

The smile faded and the blue eyes became rather acutely considering as they wandered from her disordered shining black hair released from its pins to her green eyes, to the contusions on her face, then fleetingly down her body beneath her well-cut black and white checked jacket and black skirt—both now ripped and dusty.

Finally he said thoughtfully, 'Well, now, I concede you may not be a cat burglar in disguise, but this is very definitely my bed—in fact it's my house, so for some reason you are obviously disorientated. Let's discuss that.'

Jane stared at this good-looking giant who was clad, she realised, only in a white T-shirt and underpants, and wondered if she was going mad as he returned her gaze solemnly. But as she turned her head it was *her* alarm clock that sat on the bedside table, *her* dressing-gown that hung from the door...

'No!' The word was torn from her and she tried to sit up, but her left shoulder and hip ached abominably and she sank back with a gasp.

He frowned. 'I hurt you—let me have a look.'

'Don't you touch me,' she replied through her teeth. And added, 'Look, if anyone's disorientated it's you! I've been living here for weeks! Those are my clothes hanging up in the cupboard, this is my clock—whose cosmetics do you think those are on the dressing-table?' she demanded. 'You've never seen them in your life before!'

He turned his head unhurriedly and scanned the dressing-table. 'Nice brand,' he said casually. 'Very expensive—as I happen to know, to my cost,' he added wryly. 'But I don't know if the perfume is quite your style. I would have suggested something a bit more mysterious—you could even be a Chamade girl,' he said gravely and returned his blue gaze to her. 'Yes, certainly—any girl who breaks in through windows then fights like a demented tigress deserves to be called mysterious.' And before she could react he went on imperturbably, 'OK. Let's examine how your cosmetics and things come to be in my house. By the way, allow me to introduce myself——'

But Jane had filled her lungs and would not be denied. 'I was not breaking in! I merely happened to have locked myself *out*—those are also my keys lying on the kitchen table, my car in the garage and I'll tell you why I fought like a…as I did.' She sat up this time, ignoring the pain, so great was her chagrin and anger. '*You* leapt on me like a demented Maori monster when there should have been no one in the house and only m-minutes,' she stammered, 'after I'd been chased up the street by two louts— I hate men!' she finished disjointedly but with great feeling, and she dug her hand into the tissue box beside the bed and blew her nose also with a great deal of feeling and because she was afraid she was about to cry. 'I've had the worst day you can imagine,' she went on bitterly. 'Bloody men again, if you really want to know! And now you're trying to tell me it's your house! Well, it just won't wash, mister, and I'm going to call the police.'

'I see.' It was said very seriously and the blue eyes she was staring so angrily and bitterly into betrayed only polite concern.

'Oh!' Jane groaned and fell back on the pillows but there was more to be got out of her system, she discovered, although she didn't attempt to sit up to say it. 'And how come you know so much about cosmetics and perfumes?' she shot at him as if it could only be a suspiciously wicked knowledge in her estimation—which she gave no lie to by adding contemptuously, 'Are you into women as a hobby?'

One eyebrow was raised quizzically at her, then it was again with utter gravity that he replied, 'As a hobby— no, I wouldn't say so, but I do know that most women love expensive cosmetics and as a gift they generally go down rather well. Did someone give you yours?'

'I'd *throw* them in their teeth if they did,' Jane said, again through hers, and was rewarded this time with a blink of something like surprise, but it was a short-lived victory.

'Well, remind me not to make that mistake,' her uninvited house guest said softly. 'Are you a furs and jewellery girl, then? I really didn't mean to sound cheap, you know.'

This time, he rendered her speechless. Which he took advantage of to say, 'I was about to introduce myself— I can't help feeling it might bring some clarity to our situation. I'm Liam Benedict—how do you do?' He held out his hand to her.

But Jane's mouth fell open and her eyes widened incredulously.

'Ah, I was right,' Liam Benedict murmured. 'You've heard of me.'

'I...I...' Jane floundered for words and at the same time felt like a stranded fish lying back with this man in his underwear sitting beside her being polite—and laughing at her beneath his breath, this particular man. 'I...but you're supposed to be in New Zealand doing heaven knows what,' she said feebly. But added tartly, 'Practising your Maori *haka*, obviously!'

'I don't know about that,' he said with a quizzically raised eyebrow, 'but I certainly was in New Zealand until a few hours ago. I—er—decided to come home early,' he added placidly.

'Didn't it occur to you to let anyone *know* your movements—or isn't that how you operate?' she replied witheringly.

'Well, to be honest I didn't think there would be anyone to advise in this instance—in fact I still don't know who you are or why you're here, although I'm beginning to suspect. Did your sister marry my brother James, by any chance?'

'Yes,' Jane said bleakly. 'And because Amanda and I were sharing a flat and the lease was due to run out, and because it all happened so out of the blue and *because* they went on this extended honeymoon, and you were supposed to be away for months, they suggested I move in here while they were away—but it's not all your house,' she said with more spirit. 'Don't you and your brother own it together?'

'We do,' he conceded readily. 'Our parents left it to us and we've never got around to doing anything about it. You,' he paused and watched her thoughtfully, 'don't approve of your sister marrying my brother James.'

'No. I can't think of two people less suited, to be honest.'

'I see.'

'I wish you wouldn't keep saying that!' she returned with a flash of irritation.

'You *are* very honest,' he remarked with a faint smile.

'And you're not in the least like your brother,' she retorted.

'Well, no. Are you much like your sister?' he enquired.

Jane grimaced. 'Not at all—what made you suspect I was?'

'Amanda's sister? James—er—mentioned you once.'

She raised her eyebrows. 'It must have been a pretty accurate description.'

'In some respects,' he agreed.

'Well—tell me,' she insisted in a goaded sort of voice.

Liam Benedict shrugged his broad shoulders. 'Clever, a fine enquiring mind, someone you could have a sensible discussion with about anything—what's the matter?' He looked genuinely concerned suddenly. 'Look I must have hurt you; let——'

'No, it wasn't that,' she said rather breathlessly.

'Then . . . ?'

'It was nothing—I don't see how you could possibly have recognised me from that,' she added scathingly.

He looked at her consideringly. 'Oddly, I'd be surprised if he was wrong, but he did mention something else. That you were a dark-haired, green-eyed beauty,' he said simply.

Jane laughed and discovered that it hurt for more reasons than one—her ribs were now aching as well.

'And didn't it occur to you that there *was* someone living in the house?' she said to cover it. 'I presume they forgot to advise you of the new arrangement?'

'I was dead tired when I arrived. I assumed,' he gestured towards the dressing-table and cupboard, 'those were Amanda's things, but now we've sorted all that out will you tell me your name? I can't remember it if James mentioned it——'

'It's Jane Mathieson,' she broke in wearily. 'Just plain Jane.'

'Plain?' He looked down at her wryly and took her breath away by what he said next, which was, 'You're being very brave, plain Jane, but I know your left shoulder and left hip are hurting like hell, you have a bruised jaw——' and another disfigurement you're going to like even less, he thought, but decided to keep the knowledge to himself for the time being '—your ribs might be bruised too and we're going to do something about it.'

'You—no, you're not—but how did you know?' She bit her lip.

'From my school sporting days,' he said wryly. 'And the first thing we should do is get you out of your top clothes.'

Half an hour later, to her considerable surprise—but it had been like fighting to no purpose at all—her 'top clothes' and tattered tights had been removed, she was lying on several towels in her slip, cocooned in a duvet from another bed with makeshift icebags on her hip and shoulder and holding a wrapped up block of ice to her jaw.

It was obvious from the way her green eyes were still smouldering that she yet resented this invasion of her privacy even on behalf of her health, even though she really couldn't fault the clinically dispassionate and quite gentle way he'd done it all.

She'd made two comments during the process—two that had been articulate enough for him to take into account at least. The first had been furiously to recommend that he put some clothes on, which he'd done agreeably enough—a pair of jeans and an enormous woolly jumper; the second to say equally angrily that she couldn't understand why he wasn't a doctor instead of his brother James, but somehow her grudging acknowledgement of his skilled handling of her body—in a purely nursing sense—had slipped out. And he had made no attempt to remove her full slip but had felt her hip through it quite impersonally. And he allowed her to start the process of painfully removing her tights.

He also now reappeared with a tray in his hands which he set down on the bedside table with two gently steaming cups of tea and a plate of biscuits.

'How long,' Jane said arctically, 'do I have to stay like this?'

'The longer, the better.' He pulled up a chair. 'There are two golden rules for sporting injuries: ice and support——'

'You're not proposing to swathe me in bandages, I hope? And this was not a sporting injury,' she said, articulating very precisely.

His blue eyes were peacefully amused. 'Well, no, but the same rules apply for most. But tomorrow, although I don't think there's anything serious, you should go and see your doctor.'

Jane's eyebrows shot up. 'And what should I tell him? That I ran into a Maori warrior?'

He even had beautiful teeth, she noticed, as they flashed in a contagious grin. 'Dear me, I didn't realise I'd perfected it that well, but I have spent a bit of time in New Zealand over the years and I do have many Kiwi friends.'

'How lucky you are to be able to roam backwards and forwards over the Tasman like that,' Jane said sweetly.

He narrowed his eyes faintly but then said merely, 'Why don't you have your tea? I'll help you sit up.' He piled the pillows up and simply put his hands about her waist and moved her up and readjusted the ice-bags, removing the one she was clutching to her jaw before reframing her snugly in the duvet with her hands free. Then he handed her her cup and saucer and offered her a biscuit.

Jane shook her head but sipped the tea.

He put the plate back and sat down and said seriously, 'I think you should eat more.'

She choked on some tea. 'Why?'

'To get some more flesh on your bones,' he replied mildly. 'I could pick you up with one hand.'

'Who cares?' She glared at him.

He shrugged.

'Look,' she said tautly, 'I'm sorry I don't conform to your standards of feminine perfection, but I'm quite happy the way I am—anyway, I wasn't born to be buxom.'

'I didn't say that——'

'Say what?' she flashed.

'That my standards of feminine perfection are necessarily buxom——'

'They'd need to be—they'd be smothered otherwise,' she replied contemptuously.

'Ah.' He put his cup down and regarded her with that not quite hidden laughter once more. 'I have a technique for that. I'll tell you about it if you like; it's——'

'Don't bother,' she broke in with a faint tinge of colour rising in her cheeks, and as she felt it she closed her eyes impatiently.

'If you didn't bait me I mightn't rise to it,' he said softly.

Her sweeping dark lashes flew up. 'You...'

'I was merely observing,' he said placidly, 'that you seem to be slightly underweight to me, but then very tense people often are—no, don't try to sit up,' he advised kindly. 'You'll only burn up more kilojoules unnecessarily.'

She subsided, but fuming. 'If I appear to you to be an underweight neurotic at the moment, it's not without cause. And for your information, you appear to me to be a veritable mountain of all brawn and no brain!'

He laughed. He actually laughed with amused appreciation, and Jane could only close her eyes and clench her teeth. But he murmured, 'Let's see. Your job must be—hell?'

'No, it's not. I love it—*today* was difficult, today has been one of those days,' she said with irony.

'Then what has caused you to lose weight?' he enquired quizzically.

She opened her eyes again with a frown. 'How...?'

'Your skirt was done up with a pin because it was too big for you round the waist—now,' he said meditatively, 'you don't look like the kind of girl who normally pins herself up, nor could you have lost that amount of weight in a day so—is it some man you're eating your heart out for?' For once there was a direct, sober enquiry in his eyes.

Jane found that for a stunned moment she couldn't tear her green gaze away and when she did she licked her lips before saying, without much conviction, 'No.' And she added a little wildly, 'Why are we having this crazy conversation?'

'It's probably one of the consequences of meeting as we did,' he said wryly. 'That kind of precipitate, very physical first encounter does away with a lot of conventions, don't you think? I'm glad,' he continued, 'apart from hurting you—quite unintentionally, may I say again, and apologise for?—but I'm glad that we did break some conventions, because I have the feeling it would have taken a lot of time to do it any other way. Very uptight people are often hard to get to know.'

Jane registered and digested all this with several blinks and frowns as well as making a confused mental note that she might have underestimated Liam Benedict, and finally she said cautiously, 'I don't think we need to get to know each other that well.'

For just an instant, as she stared at him, she thought she saw a fleeting look of irony cross his eyes but then they were an innocent blue and she wondered if she'd imagined it.

They remained an innocent blue as he allowed them to wander over the shadowed ivory skin of her throat and neck, the swath of hair like rough black silk that lay on her shoulder, the bruises darkening on her delicate skin, then back to her puzzled green eyes before he said, 'Well, we are relations of a sort by marriage now and I don't see why you shouldn't stay here until James and Amanda get back—there's plenty of room and you probably have a certain squatter's right, anyway. You're also going to feel pretty stiff and sore for a couple of days, so it could come in handy to have a housemate. By the way, the two louts who chased you up the road, I think we should do something about them—I have a friend in the police force. We'll give him a ring in the morning.'

CHAPTER TWO

BY NINE o'clock the next morning, Jane was once again fuming, and not only because of a very uncomfortable night but because the whole ridiculous situation she now found herself in was as flattening as an encounter with an amiable steam-roller.

Their first disagreement had sprung up when he'd brought her breakfast and innocently enquired how she felt.

'Terrible, thank you,' she replied coldly, her eyes widening as she saw his breakfast offering. Bacon and egg, two slices of toast and fruit juice. 'I can't eat all that! I don't eat breakfast—where did you get bacon and eggs, anyway?'

'Then it's time you started,' Liam Benedict said mildly. 'I walked around to the shop. You don't seem to keep much in the larder.' Once again he lifted her into a sitting position and added, 'You're probably looking forward to getting out of your petticoat—if you eat up like a good girl, I'll help you to the shower. The doctor's coming in about an hour.'

'The... what doctor?' she asked incredulously.

'A friend of mine——'

'Someone else you sponge off, I suppose!'

He sat back and looked at her pensively. 'Now I wonder what makes you say that.'

She eyed him frostily. 'Your brother James.'

He raised an eyebrow. 'James suggested to you that I sponge off people?'

For a moment Jane looked flustered. 'He—well he tried to make a joke of it but when it all came up—me moving in et cetera—he told me about you—that he had an older brother, at least,' she corrected herself, 'and—er—gave me to understand...' She stopped. 'Well, he said, with quite some irritation, believe me, that you liked to do your own thing, if you *must* know, that you were a hard person to pin down and heaven alone knew what you were doing in New Zealand but you had plenty of friends to take care of you so he guessed you'd survive. He also said that if it weren't for you,' her voice rose as a look of lazy amusement crossed Liam Benedict's good-looking face, 'he'd have sold the house ages ago!'

'Which you took to indicate—what?' he enquired quizzically.

'It indicated to me,' Jane replied with brutal candour, 'that you're some sort of good-looking, lazy layabout who drifts around the world sponging off people and he'd rather not let you get your hands on any proceeds from this house because you would blow it all—on,' she gestured, 'whatever lazy layabouts blow their money on. Wine, women and...horses, probably,' she finished disgustedly.

Liam Benedict laughed. 'That's the usual thing,' he agreed.

'So you're not denying it?' she countered.

'Well, it is because of me he hasn't sold the house,' he said gravely. 'But to get back to the doctor, he's actually a bit of a sports medicine specialist and, although yours aren't sporting injuries *of course*, you'll like him.'

'I——'

'Jane, your breakfast is getting cold,' he said softly, 'nor does it become you to pout like a spoilt brat.'

She stared up at him with her lips parted and arrested green fire in her eyes, totally transfixed and further stunned when he sat down on the side of the bed and handed her her knife and fork. 'I've been trying to work out how old you are,' he went on conversationally. 'Not that easy because sometimes you look about eighteen but when you open your mouth you often give a different impression—as if you've been around for a long time and not that happily. Here——' he took the knife and fork back, deftly cut and impaled some bacon, a bit of egg and handed the fork to her '—try it.'

She tried it, still mesmerised, but when it looked as if he was going to feed her mouthful by patient mouthful she came to life and snatched the knife and fork back. 'I can do it!'

He sat back. 'Good! The police sergeant I mentioned is coming round to have a chat with you later too.'

Jane groaned. 'Have you got any more friends you're bringing in to see me?'

'Not today,' he said with a grin. 'You haven't told me.'

'Told you what?' she said with her mouth full and her mind registering that she'd always enjoyed bacon and eggs and perhaps she should make more of an effort to eat breakfast.

'How old you are.'

'I don't see what possible bearing it can have! I'm *not* a child and I don't give a damn whether you think I pout like a spoilt brat,' she said vigorously and polished off the last bit of bacon.

'All right—that wasn't so bad, was it?' he enquired, removing the plate and offering her the second slice of toast.

'It was . . . it was very nice,' Jane said grudgingly, 'but no more toast, thanks.' Then with a spurt of irritation she added, 'Do you always get your own way?'

He stood up. 'Quite often.'

She lay back and looked at him thoughtfully. He seemed to tower over the bed, but although his shoulders were so broad, his torso, today in jeans and a fine-knit shirt, had not a spare ounce of flesh on it, and she winced, remembering suddenly how hard and honed it had felt against hers. He also didn't look quite as peaceable as he had last night, she realised, and wondered if he'd been more tired than she'd guessed. Because there was definitely something very alert in his blue eyes as he returned her gaze. Alert and quizzical, damn him, she thought, as if I really was behaving like a spoilt child—well . . .

'Would you do me a favour, Mr Benedict? Would you leave me alone for a little while?' she said with palpable irritation. 'I'm *not* a morning person at the best of times and I don't need any help to get to the shower.'

'Very well, Plain Jane Mathieson,' he said easily and picked up the tray. 'But don't be too proud to ask for help if you need it, will you?'

He went out, closing the door behind him, and Jane glared at it for a couple of moments then raised her eyes frustratedly to the ceiling. But her frustration was to grow as she started to get out of bed and realised that if she'd felt stiff and sore the night before it was nothing to how she felt now—there didn't seem to be a part of her that wasn't aching. And what was worse, the bathroom was on the other side of the central living area of the old house into which all the other rooms opened—and about all she felt capable of doing was crawling.

But she gritted her teeth, collected a loose tracksuit and fresh underwear, deliberately refrained from looking at herself in the mirror because she was quite sure she looked a fright, and, with a restrained hobble, emerged.

Liam Benedict was sitting down reading the morning paper and he glanced up, but the look she cast him should have stunned an ox and with a faint shrug he let her be.

It was with a series of restrained groans that she finally stood beneath the gush of warm water and reflected that, while ice might be great for bruises, warmth certainly seemed to help strained muscles. Thinking of the bruises, she painfully examined her hip and tried to see her shoulder and couldn't help gasping at the large and colourful nature of the ones she'd acquired. She muttered to herself that it was a miracle she hadn't broken anything and that there should be a law about letting men like Liam Benedict loose.

Then, as she finally stepped out, it occurred to her to inspect herself against his charges of being underweight, and as the steam cleared she put her hands on her waist and stared at her breasts and hips, her long slender legs— and grimaced. Her ribs weren't exactly sticking out but she had lost more weight than she'd realised, and all because...

But her train of thought was interrupted as the last of the steam cleared and she was staring at the clear reflection of her face, and for the first time taking it in— taking in the bruise on her jaw that wasn't too bad and could be covered with foundation quite easily—and the rest of it. 'I don't believe it,' she whispered. Yet close inspection proved worse. 'Oh!'

She dressed with shaking hands and more—this time heartfelt—groans, but was uncaring, and she flung the bathroom door open and leant against it. He was still sitting reading the paper and he looked up without any haste, which infuriated her all the more.

'Why didn't you tell me?' she said fiercely.

'Tell you what?' he said mildly.

'That I've got a black eye!'

'Ah.' He folded the paper precisely and put it down. 'I didn't think you'd altogether appreciate my mentioning it—I was right, but it's not that bad; I've seen far worse,' he said wryly.

'Right!' she raged, ignoring the rest of his comment. 'Don't you understand if I go into work like this, everyone will wonder...? I mean, some people might speculate——'

'That you drove some man to violence?' he speculated for her, and shrugged his magnificent shoulders. 'Depends on the kind of record you have, I'd say, but anyway there's no question of your going to work and they know it.'

'*Drove*—how dare you?' she flung at him and went still. 'What do you mean, they know it?'

'Someone from your office rang while you were asleep. I told them you'd had an accident and it might be a couple of days before you could get in.'

'And who,' she whispered, but only because her voice didn't seem to want to work properly, 'did you say you were?'

'Your new housemate,' he replied blandly. 'Now that,' he went on casually, 'did cause a bit of a stir. The girl I was talking to said something like "didn't think she had it in her!" And she sent you a message.'

Jane grabbed the door for extra support in case she fainted from sheer rage.

'She said,' her tormentor continued, 'to tell you to go for it and forget about your career for once before it was too late. A lively-sounding girl, she was.' He raised a dark eyebrow at her.

'My secretary,' Jane said through chattering teeth, 'but this time she's had it.'

'Don't you think that's a bit rough?' he murmured.

'You don't know her,' Jane retorted. 'It's all she ever thinks about, but be that as it may—you had no right to do it——'

'But you've just confirmed that you're very wary of your black eye being misunderstood, so I think I did what was best, in fact,' he drawled. And added with a trace of impatience, 'You're not silly enough to believe you could actually go to work today, are you? I thought lawyers were supposed to be very logical people.'

'How did you know I was one? Don't tell me. Laura again!'

'Well, she did begin by asking for the firm's up-and-coming lady lawyer, *Ms* Mathieson——' he grinned faintly '—but I now remember that James mentioned it. Do you intend to hang on to that door for much longer, Ms Mathieson?'

He was saved the venom of Jane's reply by the arrival of the doctor.

'Well, young lady,' his doctor friend was grey-haired and kindly, 'there is no damage other than the spectacular bruising, but time will heal all that.'

'It just happens to be the one thing I haven't got that much of,' Jane said broodingly, and laid her head back with a sigh. They were alone in her bedroom, where, to her chagrin, Liam Benedict had carried her. 'Why me? And why——' she raised her head '—him?'

The doctor looked amused. 'I gather this was how you two met.'

'Yes,' Jane confirmed feelingly. 'Why couldn't he have been a five-foot-two wimp?'

'I'm sure he wishes you'd been a six-foot Amazon; he's probably feeling very guilty.'

'He doesn't show it,' she said darkly, then remembered he was a friend and apologised. 'Sorry,' she said wearily. 'I'm not behaving very well but I don't feel very well and I have other problems on top of it all—such as finding somewhere to live,' she muttered.

The doctor rose. 'I wouldn't rush that. You might need Liam around for a couple of days.' He smiled down at her with a definite twinkle in his eye.

And on the heels of the doctor came the police sergeant— this time a hearty, exuberant man who thumped Liam repeatedly on the shoulder before, reluctantly, she felt, turning his attention to her. It was, though little did she know it, something she was going to experience often in relation to Amanda's brother-in-law, but even at this early stage in the proceedings she couldn't help being amazed at the way people seemed to be riveted at being in his company—what a con! she thought darkly.

All the same, once he did turn his attention to her, the police sergeant was thorough and kindly too and he assured her that all stops would be pulled out to catch the two young louts. And she was feeling somewhat mollified until he added, with a grin, that she probably had the best protection she could get with Liam living in the house.

She attempted to raise the subject as soon as they were alone.

'Would you like to come out and watch television?' he enquired from the bedroom doorway. 'I found a good video on the set.'

'I want...damn,' Jane said, momentarily distracted. 'It's overdue. I forgot to take it back yesterday morning.'

'Did you get to watch it?'

'No, I didn't do that either! Unlike you, I work for a living,' she added scathingly.

'Perhaps a bit too hard,' he murmured. 'But what's the problem?' he countered to her fierce expression. 'We can watch it now and pay the overdue fee. Provided one doesn't make a habit of it, it's probably what ordinary mortals do a lot.'

'Are you saying...?'

She stopped because he advanced towards her and calmly picked her up again as if she were as light as a feather. 'I'm saying you're working yourself into a state for no good reason.'

She winced, inwardly this time, partly because he might be right but also because of utter helplessness and not only, she realised, because of his strength, but also because of a little breath of memory catching her unawares. A memory of her father all those years ago and the safe feeling of his arms before he'd deserted her...

'There,' he remarked, putting her down carefully on the settee, 'what will it be?'

'Be?' She looked up at him her eyes wide.

'Do you want to watch the video or should we try to indulge in some civilised conversation?'

She tightened her mouth, but it only added to her feeling shrewish. Shrewish? How did he do it? She was the one bearing the pain he'd, even if in some misapprehension, inflicted on her. Wasn't she entitled to feel somewhat shrewish?

She was not, she realised with a little flush rising in her cheeks as their gazes held and she detected an ironical 'enough is enough, surely?' glint in his eye.

She looked away and said abruptly, 'We should talk, yes. As soon as I'm over all this, I'll be looking for somewhere to stay—I hope you don't mind putting up with me in the meantime?' Her lips moved in the semblance of a rather wry smile.

He sat down opposite. 'How long were you planning to stay here? Before I made my untimely return, that is.'

'Well,' Jane fiddled with a thread on the arm of the settee, 'James and Amanda seemed to be under the impression that you would be away for at least four months, so...' She grimaced.

'I still don't see why you should move out. It's big enough for both of us.' He gestured comprehensively.

'I...' Jane paused. 'Thank you for the offer, but I prefer living on my own—I'm sure you probably do too,' she said with a faint smile.

'Why?'

She stared at him. 'Why what?'

'Do you prefer living on your own?' he said patiently.

She took a deep breath. 'It's not so very unnatural, is it?'

He shrugged. 'It can be lonely—unless you have a very active social life?' He raised his eyebrows at her.

'No,' she said shortly.

'And you did live with your sister, didn't you?'

'There's a big difference between a sister and *you*.'

He grinned and murmured. 'Think of me as a brother.'

'That's ridiculous.' She looked at him coldly.

'I can assure you you'd be quite safe from me. I'm not into rape.'

'I didn't imagine that,' she denied hotly.

'Oddly enough, those beautiful green eyes look at me as if that's exactly what you imagine sometimes,' he said softly. 'But, since you assure me otherwise, what further objections do you have?' He stared at her gravely.

Jane took a breath. 'Can't you see how awkward it could be for two strangers to live together? We could drive each other round the bend! Then there would undoubtedly be the problems of your love-life——'

'My love-life,' he broke in, 'is not nearly as extensive as you seem to imagine. In fact I can promise you I wouldn't embarrass you in that direction at all.' He paused. 'Is *your* love-life the problem?'

'What love-life?' Jane said cynically, and grimaced as soon as the words had left her mouth. 'Why,' she went on immediately and more forcefully, 'are you pushing this, Mr Benedict?'

'Do call me Liam.' He stood up and wandered over to the window. 'I feel a bit guilty about upsetting everyone's arrangements.' He shrugged and turned to her. 'Especially since you're part of the family now——'

'Very distantly if at all, and you do surprise me,' Jane commented drily.

'All the same, one day there'll be kids who will be our common nieces and nephews.'

Jane looked away and found that she was feeling weary and drained, and that despite her determination to do it the thought of moving yet again—it was only six months since their mother had died and she and Amanda had gone through the trauma of selling up their house and moving to an apartment—the hassle of finding somewhere, the inevitable first few weeks of loneliness and alienation before you felt at home at all, were tiring even to contemplate. I'd just started to feel at home here, she reflected, and sighed.

'Why don't we give it trial run?'

She raised her green eyes to his. 'I suppose we could do that,' she said a little helplessly.

She slept a lot during the day and spent the rest of the time consorting with ice bags which she was only too happy to discard when, after leaving her alone for most of the day, Liam Benedict appeared at her bedroom doorway and enquired whether she felt well enough to get up to eat dinner with him.

'You're very domesticated,' she commented, and accepted.

But when she sat down at the table carefully, she discovered his meal consisted of Chinese take-away food.

'Not that domesticated,' he said to her raised eyebrows. 'How about you?'

'Not that domesticated either,' she confessed. 'Amanda is,' she added drily.

'So you got the brains. Does she look like you?'

'I didn't say she was brainless!'

His lips twitched. 'Your tone of voice seemed to imply it.'

'I... Didn't James tell you about her?' Jane queried, changing tack.

'No. All I got was the news that he'd married an absolute honey, and an admonition to eat my heart out.'

For a moment a glint of contempt lit Jane's eyes but she veiled them immediately and said in a colourless voice, 'She is in fact a honey-blonde, she's five-foot-nothing, she's quite scatter-brained in some respects—she would not have the slightest idea how to fill in her own tax form—but she's also warm and cuddly, she's a cuddler and a toucher herself and it's impossible not to be warmed and charmed in her presence.' She stared at a forkful of honeyed prawn then put it into her mouth slowly.

'None of which you are, I gather,' Liam Benedict said with a grin. 'But I don't see why she shouldn't make a good wife. You might be the one with problems in that regard.'

'Obviously,' Jane said, and chose some beef in black bean sauce for her next mouthful.

'Did you want him yourself, Jane?'

It was said softly but the effect on Jane was electric. She spilled black bean sauce down the top of her tracksuit and choked on what little beef had made it to her mouth.

To make matters worse, Liam went on thoughtfully after offering to bang her on the back, 'I could have saved you a lot of heartache if I'd been here. James would never have done for you because, despite his brains, he's really a soft touch underneath and you would have walked all over him, whereas Amanda, by the sound of it, will make him feel like the lord of the manor. I think they'll do very well. What, as a matter of interest,' his gaze rested on her still flushed face, 'got to you about James? Did his apparent intellectualism make you think he was the kind of man who could offer you mental stimulation and the rest of it would fall into place?'

Jane swallowed several times to make sure she could trust her voice. 'What makes you think you can read me like an open book, Mr Benedict?' she said finally. 'You've made an amazing number of assumptions on the basis of less than twenty-four hours' acquaintance.'

He half smiled. 'True, but, as I mentioned before, the manner of our getting to know each other has been such that a lot of the restrictions one normally displays have been dispensed with. In other words, your extreme gall led you into giving a lot of things away, Jane. I also happen to know he met you first and was quite taken with you, at first. His letter indicated as much. I gather that he either then got to know you better or met your warm, cuddly sister—or both—and, to your dismay and disapproval, fell for her like a ton of bricks. Men,' he said meditatively, 'like to be touched, so, if it happens to you again, remember that. They're also pretty fond of their egos, alas.'

'Yes, well,' Jane said, having difficulty articulating, 'I doubt if I've ever met a more monumental ego than yours.'

'Ah, but it's also much tougher than my brother's.'

'And I've *no* doubt you much prefer to be touched than mentally stimulated,' she said mockingly.

'Of course the ideal,' he drawled, 'is a fine mix of the two. But the fact that she can't fill in a tax form doesn't mean they don't have their own special level of mental stimulation. Haven't you had much luck with sex, Jane?'

Two sets of thoughts crossed Jane's mind. It occurred to her to wonder what sex with Liam Benedict would be like. A dizzying, rapturous event? Certainly a very vulnerable event, she decided, gazing at him. You would very definitely be at the mercy of his humour because physically—well, she already knew what it was like to tangle with him physically. And psychologically? Psychologically, you don't appear to be much of a match for him either, she reflected with a grimace. Then it occurred to her that she'd spent years of virtually blood, sweat and tears getting her law degree and she should be able to do better against him than she had so far, even if he was blessed with a considerable degree of acuteness, not to mention second sight. After all, the man was an unemployed drifter, wasn't he?

She said, 'That's none of your business. But I'd like to set the record straight in some respects. I love my sister despite occasionally getting exasperated with her. The other thing is, I don't think the prospect of any amount of common nieces and nephews gives you the right to ask me questions like your last one.'

He lifted a lazy eyebrow. 'I do have a vested interest in this marriage, however. So should you.'

'I'm certainly not going to do anything to tear it apart,' she said deliberately.

'You didn't hide how you felt very well from me.'

Jane took a breath and forced herself to smile at him. 'Do you know something? I've got this funny feeling fate arranged for you to enter my life for the express purpose of tormenting me. Look, it's over. If I did think of James in that context and if I can't help wondering if my sister won't bore him to tears in ten years' time— with an element of pique, yes,' she conceded with a little glint in her eyes, 'I'll recover, trust me. As for them,' she said with a glint of humour this time, 'the rest of the world might not exist.'

'So Amanda didn't realise she was stealing your boy-friend?' he queried.

'Amanda has formed the impression that I'm allergic to the opposite sex, probably because I'm not the cuddly type as you so perceptively *gathered* yourself. But she did ask me if I was seriously interested, she did do that.'

'And you retired gracefully.'

'I retired hurt,' Jane said after a moment. 'Your brother...' she added slowly, then shrugged. 'I liked him.'

There was a few minutes' silence during which she finished her meal and awkwardly began gathering plates.

'Leave that,' Liam said. 'You'll probably be more comfortable on the settee. You know, I think James would have bored *you* in ten years' time.'

'Perhaps.' She shrugged wearily. Then she said irritably, 'This *conversation* is becoming quite boring, you know. It's not even as if I'd got to the stage of deciding I might fall in love with him. It could even have been a general sense of jealousy—Amanda has always had men running after her.'

'Whereas you have always scared them silly. Tell you what, Jane,' he said thoughtfully, capturing her gaze, 'you don't scare me.'

She blinked. 'Do you mean...? No,' she said on a startled breath, then more forcefully, 'You, because of your sheer size, are in the fortunate position of not having to be scared by much at all!'

'I meant,' he drawled, 'that despite your academic qualifications, despite your way with words and your hostility towards me, you remind me very much of a furious kitten. Would you like coffee or tea?' He stood up with an enquiring glance.

For a moment, to her horror, Jane felt like nothing so much as a spitting, furious kitten—an analogy that should have filled the feminist part of her soul with utter contempt. 'I,' she said shakily, 'don't see what on earth that's got to do with anything!'

'You don't?' He smiled faintly and his blue eyes were slightly ironic. 'It has a lot to do with our process of——' he paused '—getting to know each other,' he finished blandly. 'In other words, you might as well relax and draw in your claws. You're only tiring yourself out. Coffee or tea? Or would you like a drink? That might help.'

'Getting to know each other,' she repeated rather dazedly. 'What do you mean?'

He studied her bruised, upturned face for a long moment. 'I mean,' he said finally, 'that *I* think fate might have thrown us together because we could be eminently more suited than you and James, or anyone else who comes to mind for that matter. We both enjoy a contest, obviously. We are both unattached and your problems with touching and cuddling might be solved quite simply by the right stimulus—in fact your battered ego could receive just the boost it needs from an affair with me. But before you start jumping *out* of windows, dear Jane, I will never *force* you to come to bed with me—I only repeat myself in the interests of your health.' And with the lightest careless touch of his fingers on her cheek, he walked away.

CHAPTER THREE

JANE stared after Liam with her mouth open and her heart beating most erratically.

He didn't go far. They'd eaten at the kitchen table and he'd filled the kettle and reached up for a bottle of brandy by the time she managed to say uncertainly, 'I don't believe this.'

What he would have replied she was never to know because the phone on the counter beside him rang and he picked it up.'

Jane didn't take in much of the one-sided conversation that ensued. She was still stunned to a degree that amazed her. So when he put it down and said to her, 'You'll like young Sam. Did James mention him?' she had no idea what he was talking about.

'Sam?' she said confusedly.

'He's our cousin. He's nineteen, and, having discovered I'm home and seeing he's on vacation from university, he's invited himself to stay for a few weeks.'

'Stay?'

Liam splashed a generous tot of brandy into a glass and rummaged through a cupboard for soda. 'Do you mind? Perhaps I should have asked you.'

'It's your house,' Jane heard herself say.

He brought the drink over to her. 'Try that. So it is. But from your point of view, if you're still worried, there could be safety in numbers,' he said musingly.

Jane took the glass and took a large swallow. 'Tell me something,' she said huskily. 'Why?'

The doorbell rang.

His lips twitched and he seemed about to say something then he changed his mind and went to answer it.

It was Laura.

'Jane!' She advanced upon her boss but not until she'd exchanged a good few moments of pleasantries with Liam Benedict that had clearly indicated her first impressions of him were favourable. She'd even said, 'My God! Are you who I think you are? Are *you* Jane's new housemate? Strike me pink!'

'Jane,' she said now—Laura was another honey-blonde, a divorcee in her thirties, very smart, very into men and very outspoken, 'darling, what on earth happened to you?'

'*Mr* Benedict here,' Jane said precisely, 'thought I was a burglar and attacked me and did this to me.' And now he wants to have an affair with me, she thought, her precision reverting to her former state of confusion.

'But——'

Jane made another effort. 'He also happens to be my sister's brother-in-law, he's supposed to be overseas, he didn't know I had moved into this house that he owns jointly with James—which was how the confusion arose——'

'Helped along by the fact that she entered by the window,' Liam said gravely.

'Only because I'd locked my keys inside—and until he all but broke every bone in my body we had never laid eyes on one another!' Jane finished in rising tones and rising awkwardly herself only to be utterly incensed by the glances Liam and Laura exchanged. 'Oh!'

'Yes, well,' Liam said then, and, coming round the table, picked her up and took her into the lounge where he deposited her gently on the settee with her legs stretched out, and placed some cushions behind her, 'I didn't break any bones,' he said over his shoulder to Laura, who had followed these proceedings avidly, 'but Jane is pretty bruised and battered, and really feeling it at the moment, I would say.'

'If you pick me up without my permission just once more, Liam Benedict, I shall...I shall scream,' Jane threatened furiously.

'Jane,' Laura stared at her, 'are you out of your—I was going to say tiny mind but no one could accuse you of that—are you out of your mind? I would give my eye-teeth to be in your position, darling.' She turned a witty, provocative glance upon Liam and added candidly, 'You have to be the dishiest hunk I've seen for years!'

Jane cast her eyes heavenwards. 'How do you know he's not as thick as a block of wood?' she said through her teeth, and added, 'Laura, if you go back to work and spread rumours or innuendoes about *housemates* or even tell anyone I've got a black eye, I shall get myself another secretary. Why are you here, anyway?'

Laura didn't answer. Instead she said over Jane's head to Liam, 'Are you sure you didn't give her serious concussion, Mr Benedict?'

'I wondered that myself but the doctor thinks not. I believe our Ms Mathieson is rather uptight generally, that's all,' Liam Benedict said consideringly.

'As a matter of fact, we've all been wondering when she'd burn herself out,' Laura said slowly as Jane's mouth fell open. 'She got her degree part-time, you know. That's doing it the hard way—five years as an articled clerk with night school and she did it in five years when it should have taken six—and since she qualified, well, I don't know if you know how the system

works but law firms operate on budgets and even the
most fledgeling newcomer is expected to make the budget
they're assigned. Believe me, I've seen not a few burn
themselves out in the process, especially the women, and,
to make matters worse, Jane's a nervy sort of type too.'

Jane made an odd sort of strangled sound and they
both looked down at her then went on discussing her as
if she wasn't there. 'Oh, she's rather brilliant,' Laura
said generously.

'I believe you,' Liam commented. 'Do you think she's
having some sort of nervous breakdown?'

'Well——'

I don't believe this, Jane thought chaotically.

'Well,' Laura said again, 'tell you what, this could
have happened most fortuitously, Liam.' She smiled at
him brilliantly. 'A week or ten days off could be just
what she needs and you've provided her with the perfect
excuse to take it and with no broken bones either, and
with you here to look after her, what's more! Jane, love,'
she turned her attention to the settee, 'all I'm going to
say back at work is that there's no chance of your coming
in for at least a week. On every other aspect, I shall
maintain a discreet silence, you may rely on me. And
I'll pop off now. I'm sure you'll be able to handle her,
Liam,' she said with another dazzling smile.

'Here.'

Jane opened her eyes, which she'd closed as Laura
left, to see Liam offering her her drink. She took it
mutely and stayed mute until he came back with one for
himself and cast himself down in the armchair opposite
and put his long legs up on a stool.

'Cheers,' he said with a grin. 'She's probably right, you know. A break might be just what you need and a legitimate break can't do your career any harm, can it?'

Jane breathed deeply and took a sip of brandy. 'No.'

'Provided you can relax, of course.'

She laid her head back. 'Of course. Right at this moment it looks like a distinct impossibility, I have to tell you, but I'll work on it.'

'Why don't you have a good cry?' he suggested. 'It seems to work wonders with women.'

'Do you know, I honestly wish I could? But I don't think I'm that sort of woman either. And how you expect me to relax,' she sat up, suddenly remembering, 'after telling me you intend to con me into having an affair with you, I can't really imagine,' she added bitterly. 'Why?'

'Why what?'

'Why me? Have I hurt your pride by telling you some home truths?''

'Which ones?' he queried.

'Which...?' She took a frustrated breath. 'Well, I thought I'd made it quite obvious I don't approve of your lifestyle, I've cast aspersions on your mental abilities——'

'Oh, that,' he said amiably. 'No. I think I'm immune to it,' he added, slipping down in the chair and making himself lazily comfortable.

'Then *why*?'

He looked across at her wryly. 'Who knows? That's the kind of question wise men never try to answer, I'm told.' He ran his hand through his hair and shrugged. 'I guess physically you must appeal to me. In fact, physically you're almost a work of art, or will be when you recover.' He gazed at her thoughtfully. 'I've never seen anyone look quite so attractive with a black eye and you still have the most exquisite skin and hair like midnight, long legs and a figure that's nearly perfect, I would imagine—you're blushing,' he said idly.

'I'm also a neurotic shrew, in your estimation,' she pointed out with an effort.

'I think I could change that,' he said softly. 'There is a very well-known precedent, talking in legal terms, for that kind of metamorphosis.'

Jane narrowed her eyes. 'If we're also talking of Shakespeare and *his* famous shrew, believe me, she'd leave me for dead, so your talents in that direction could be quite wasted—apart from the fact that they're going to be wasted anyway.'

'Tell me about this aversion and allergy you have to men, apart from my brother James,' he said lightly.

'I don't *have* an aversion to men——'

'But last night you were extremely vocal on the subject of "bloody" men. Men at work, men who chased you down the street—that I can understand——'

'Thank you,' Jane said acidly.

'And me,' he continued unperturbed.

'If you can't understand why I have an aversion to *you*, you must be dumber than I gave you credit for!'

He merely smiled slightly.

'Of course,' she said coldly, 'the way some females appear to fawn over you has to take some of the credit for your inflated ego but I should warn you not to set too much store by Laura; she's only one and she's man-crazy.'

'Thank *you*,' he said.

Jane made an angry little sound and took refuge in her drink. But she still felt unreasonably het up, she discovered, and wondered why. 'Men do get on my nerves sometimes,' she said more to herself than him. 'But isn't that fairly natural between the sexes? I mean, I'm not really a man-hater but yesterday was one of those days when all those I dealt with seemed to be smugly superior about something, and if you must know,' she paused, 'it did occur to me that I was having to do two strokes to their one to keep my head above water, and, what's more, if I'd *been* a man, I'd probably have been able to fix my car, I'd have been able to drive to work and consequently drive home instead of having to take a bus and get chased down the road, I wouldn't have locked myself out—and I wouldn't be in this ridiculous position,' she said broodingly.

'What's wrong with your car?'

'It just wouldn't start.'

'I'll have a look at it in the morning.'

'Do you know anything about cars?'

'A bit.'

'Do you own a car?' she queried with unconscious hauteur.

'Not at the moment, no.'

'How do you plan to get about, then?'

'I wasn't planning to get about much for a while,' he said mildly. 'But Sam does own a car so it shouldn't be a problem if I need to.'

'How convenient,' Jane murmured, her eyes scornful.

'It is, isn't it?' he replied equitably and added softly, 'Not that I imagine you approve for a moment. You might have made a good schoolteacher too, Jane.'

She looked up and disturbed a wicked little glint of amusement in his eyes. But instead of taking umbrage she sighed, then, to her amazement, found she was laughing. 'Perhaps I do need a break,' she said at last.

'You're even more beautiful when you laugh.'

'Am I?' She sobered and lay back. 'I'm also a twenty-four-year-old spinster who's very set in her ways, so——'

'From conscious choice, religious beliefs, lack of the right man?'

She said nothing for a long time. 'From lack of something, perhaps.'

He pushed himself up in his chair and studied her with a faint frown. 'But not completely inexperienced, Jane?'

She grimaced and wondered how to answer for several reasons—it was none of his business whether she was a virgin to start with and suddenly her inexperience was a slightly sore point, she discovered to her amazement, because it made her feel inadequate and rather vulnerable. So she said cryptically, 'Would that I were, I sometimes think.' And comforted herself with the thought that it was only a little white lie and also that none of the few occasions she'd been kissed had left her with a burning desire to repeat it.

'So your experiences of sex *haven't* been very satisfactory,' he said with a twist of her lips.

Jane surprised herself at this point. 'Your preoccupation with my sex life is a little bizarre, surely?' she drawled.

'I'm confused, that's all,' he said lazily. 'You *say* you have nothing against men, yet a lot of your other observations on the subject seem to contradict that.'

'All right, I'll enlighten you—in the hope that we can put this riveting topic to bed. What an unfortunate choice of words,' she marvelled before he could comment. 'To me men *are* rivals, I suppose you could say, due, probably, to some of the reasons I outlined before, but it's not only in a work-related context that they like to be superior, it's the bedroom too. I just don't take kindly to it,' she said ingenuously.

He laughed softly. 'I can imagine. Ah, well, that too could change one day, but before you have a seizure let's change the subject. Why such a burning desire to succeed at such cost—I mean, being in danger of burning yourself out?'

'I don't really know,' she said slowly, then something that had been bothering her throughout the conversation surfaced. 'You sound quite well educated.' She turned her head to him.

A dry smile twisted his lips. 'Why shouldn't I be?''

'I ... I just thought ...'' She floundered awkwardly.

'You mean you made some sweeping assumptions about me. Whatever else I lack, before I—er—became a lazy layabout, I qualified as an accountant but that was aeons ago,' he said with a charming smile.

Jane closed her mouth with a click.

'I'm sure that seems like heaping coals of fire on your head but it wasn't my intention, so don't worry about how you could apologise for certain things you've said to me or about me,' he went on.

She blushed then said stiffly, 'I do, however, apologise. But that makes it even worse—why are you throwing away your life like this?' she demanded.

'Let's just say—I got tired of the rat race.' He shrugged. 'It doesn't seem to be doing you a lot of good.'

'Yes, well, let's get back to what we were talking about before——' She broke off, blushed and bit her lip.

He considered her hot face and said, not quite smiling, 'That is being caught between the devil and the deep blue sea. What aspect of what we were discussing before would you like to tackle now? We've been through the nebulous nature of what attracts people to each other—

well, there is this,' he said with a kind of gravity she
mistrusted devoutly, 'it does get a bit tedious to be—
er—fawned over—your choice of words, I believe—so
you're certainly a bit of a novelty.'

Jane stared at him incredulously. 'And what happens
when—I mean if...?' She broke off and started again.
'Hypothetically, aren't you planning to bring me to that
state?'

Their gazes caught and a curious little shiver ran down
her spine as she read a sudden look of cool determination in his. 'I can't deny,' he said slowly, 'that the
prospect of taming you, my green-eyed shrew, has its
appeal. On the other hand, if I thought I could tame
you completely, I wouldn't be interested.'

Jane's eyes widened unevenly, her lips parted and she
found she felt exactly like someone who'd been playing
with fire unknowingly, and got burnt.

'And that,' he said drily, still watching her with that
narrowed, cool look, 'has really set the cat among the
pigeons, I gather. Are you about to hobble into your
bedroom and pack your bags? Why don't you stay and
fight on? If nothing else it will enlarge your experience
of life.'

If her eyes had ever sparked green fire at him, they
certainly did so now, but she veiled them almost immediately. 'How do I know I can trust your Queensberry
rules?' she said sardonically.

'You don't. You'll have to rely on your instincts, and
Sam when he comes.'

'He's not here at the moment,' Jane pointed out, then
bit her lip.

'Do you really imagine I'm a rapist in disguise, Jane?'
he said, and there was no mistaking the contempt in his
voice.

Did she? When it was put like that, she didn't, but it didn't make her like him any better, she decided, him or his contempt or his ambition to tame her... 'Very well,' she said tautly, 'you want a fight? You've got it.'

'Perhaps we should establish exactly what we're about to do battle over?' he drawled.

'On my side, that's quite clear and simple.' She subjected him to a slightly one-eyed green gaze. 'I do not suffer from any physical attraction to you——'

'Would you admit it if you did, Jane?' he queried gently.

She tightened her lips. 'And *I* am battling your incredible assumption that I need *you* to make me over into a state of all womanly submission—you of all people, a drifter and a drop-out,' she said scornfully. 'On the other hand, what you're battling is not quite clear to me, Mr Benedict. Forgive me for saying so but it could be something as simple as the fact that I *didn't* immediately keel over and fawn all over you, despite your protestations that your pride wasn't much hurt, and that you like me the way I am while still wanting to "tame" me—quite a contradiction, don't you think? And, by the way, if I ever do become allergic to anything it will be to that little word!'

'Bravo!' he replied. 'If you're not at the bar, you should be.'

'And you...' She stopped. 'I'm going to bed,' she said disgustedly.

'Are you? Well, I'm going to watch your video.'

'Do you mean you still haven't taken the wretched thing back?' she demanded.

'No, but I rang them and got an extension. Goodnight, Jane.' He stood up politely. 'Like a helping hand?' he asked, his eyes an innocent blue.

He was laughing at her, she knew. He was also as tough an opponent as she was ever likely to meet at the bar—even if he was a drifter and a drop-out—if she ever got there, and a man you couldn't help being intrigued by in the way that a clever enemy intrigued you... Her eyes widened at this point in her thoughts and she immediately chided herself for being oddly fanciful—extremely fanciful. She'd known him for barely twenty-four hours and during most of that time he'd enraged and outraged her.

'No. No, thank you,' she said with an odd little gesture. 'I can manage. Goodnight.'

Her waking thoughts the next morning, after sleeping like a log, to her surprise, were that she felt a lot better. She moved cautiously to test this out and found that no longer did every movement cause her pain, although she doubted she could leap about much.

Then she realised there seemed to be a lot of voices and some movement coming from the other side of her door, and a glance at her alarm clock told her it was late—half-past nine, in fact. Not that that was any reason for Liam Benedict to fill the house with visitors, particularly when she hadn't showered or had a chance to visit the bathroom—damn the man, she thought irately, and only then remembered the challenge she'd accepted last night and some of the incredible things he'd said to her.

She took a very deep breath, wondered briefly if she'd imagined it all, decided she hadn't, and rose from her bed filled with a steely determination.

She also pulled on a pair of fitted black trousers, a soft green jumper with a scoop neck that matched her eyes and hugged her figure, and stared at her face in the

mirror. Both her black eye and the bruise on her jaw
appeared to have faded slightly but even so they gave
her a rakish look she detested, she decided, and not one
she was prepared to expose to whoever her impossible
housemate had filled the place with. So she cleansed and
toned her skin with her expensive cosmetics, another sore
point, and applied a film of the luminous foundation
she used to her face. It worked on her jaw but not on
her eye which was still slightly puffy anyway. She grimaced and brushed her hair vigorously until it shone and
crackled with vitality and lay on her shoulder in a long
smooth sweep. Then in gesture of defiance she sprayed
some perfume to the base of her throat and immediately
asked herself what she thought she was doing. But
wanting to look and feel presentable was no sin, she decided. It might even give her the confidence she appeared to lack in this situation—only there was still her
black eye.

At that point her gaze fell on her sunglasses and she
thought, Of course! Why not?

In fact there was only one other person in the lounge
and all of the noise was coming from the television which
Liam flicked off lazily with the remote control. But
before either of them could say a word a young giant
with remarkably familiar blue eyes who had been
lounging on the settee bounded up and came over to her.
'You must be Jane. Wow!' This was said with reverence,
then, 'Liam's told me about you only he forgot to say
how simply gorgeous you were. I'm Sam. How do you
do? I'm really impressed, Liam,' he added over his
shoulder.

Jane glared at him then removed her glasses to give
it more effect and said icily, 'Impressed about what?'

'Well——' Sam's eyes widened and he glanced at his cousin again then back at Jane, but Liam spoke.

'I forgot to mention Jane is not a morning person, Sam; sorry,' he said idly.

The cumulative effect of all this caused Jane to grope for the bedroom door-handle, and, in a sudden excess of emotion and frustration, take a step into the lounge and slam the door closed so that it rocked on its hinges. Then she wished she'd slammed herself into her bedroom instead of the other way round because she was left in the lounge with not one but two almost perfect specimens of masculinity staring at her gravely and in the universally male manner that hid an inner amusement at the vagaries of the female sex.

'If you dare laugh at me—either of you,' she warned through her teeth, 'I'll start throwing things. What have you been telling him?' she demanded of Liam.

It was Sam who responded. 'Nothing, nothing,' he hastened to assure her. 'Well, very little actually,' he amended. 'I just jumped to the wrong conclusion when I saw you,' he said earnestly and smiled suddenly at her. 'Can I get you a cup of tea? My mother always says she's good for nothing until she's had a cup of tea in the morning.'

Jane closed her eyes because Liam Benedict's cousin was about as irresistible as a very friendly overgrown Great Dane puppy. 'Thank you...I...yes, that would be nice. I'll just...go to the bathroom. I do hope you'll take the opportunity to set the record quite straight in the meantime,' she couldn't resist adding to Liam, however, with considerable irony.

A little glint disturbed the placid blue of his eyes. 'Of course. By the way, I got your car going.'

She compressed her lips then marched across the room, tossing her head.

When she emerged, breakfast was in the process of being prepared, a huge breakfast, she saw, of bacon, sausages and scrambled eggs, and she said involuntarily, 'Thank God I don't have to pay your food bills, Sam.'

Sam smiled at her engagingly and pulled out a chair for her. 'My mum says it's like feeding an army. Here's your tea.'

'I feel I must have a lot in common with your mum, Sam. Thank you. What——' she glanced towards the stove where Liam was pricking sausages '—was wrong with my car, as a matter of interest?'

'Nothing much. A bit of gunk on the battery terminals. I see you're feeling a lot better this morning. Physically.'

Jane tossed her head but replied brightly, 'Yes, I am. My mental condition, incidentally, was induced by the noise of the television. It sounded to me as if you had invited an army to breakfast. I am as yet unused to people who begin the day by watching videos,' she explained sweetly. 'Didn't you get to see it all last night?'

He turned from the sausages at last. 'No, I fell asleep watching it. But since I'll be paying for it, I decided that not to watch it through would be a waste of money. I wonder if I'm turning over a new leaf?' he mused wryly.

Jane pursed her lips and wondered why she got the distinct impression she was being made fun of. She also, as she studied him, remembered her surprising thoughts about the intriguing kind of enemy Liam Benedict made—remembered them with a curious little inward shiver of apprehension. Yet he didn't look that dangerous this morning, wearing jeans and his mulberry sweater again with his eyes very blue and his dark hair brushed and tidy—mainly, she decided, because that cool determination of last night wasn't evident. Had she imagined it?

Perhaps some of what she was thinking showed in her eyes because he smiled suddenly and in a way that reminded her of Sam, and said, 'I'm very pleased and relieved to see you looking so much better, you know. I've told Sam how it all came about and he reckons I should be shot——' Sam broke in to say fervently that he should have been more careful anyway '—but I can still make amends of another kind. None of us has got much on over the next week, so why don't we enjoy each other's company—we are family of a kind after all—take a few outings, be lazy if we feel like it—that kind of thing?'

'What a good idea!' Sam said ingenuously and turned to Jane with glowing enthusiasm. 'Please say yes. With you here the time will go much faster, I'm sure!'

'I . . .' Jane lifted her gaze to Liam's but his was again that innocent blue that now spoke volumes to her. Then she frowned. 'Why do we need the time to go quickly?'

Liam spoke before Sam could. 'I'm sure you're not looking forward to languishing around on your own with a black eye.'

Whereupon Sam opened and closed his mouth then said severely to his cousin, 'It's sacrilege, you know!'

'Oh, I quite agree,' Liam answered but with a look of amusement.

Sam opened his blue eyes at him. 'Then it is our duty to make the time go pleasantly for Jane—you're right!'

'We could certainly try,' Liam Benedict said gravely and turned back to his sausages. 'But it is *up* to Jane.'

'Jane?'

'I . . .' Jane said again, then, helplessly, 'All right.'

*   *   *

That week was something of a revelation to Jane. After her father's defection and with no brothers or uncles she'd had little to do with men and without Amanda's innate or whatever it was understanding of them, when she'd finally left her all-girls school it had been rather like going among a strange tribe.

But the two men, if Sam could be called one, who took care of that week of her life, revealed facets of the masculine gender that surprised her, sometimes delighted, sometimes exasperated her, never bored her and made her rather acutely conscious that she'd imbibed more of her mother's bitterness towards men than she'd realised. And she thought of her father a couple of times with a little pang of resentment. Not that that was new, but she was suddenly seeing more clearly what she'd missed out on.

She once tried to catalogue just what she had missed out on and came up firstly with a sense of security, which was fairly obvious, she mused. What wasn't so obvious was the different sense of humour that permeated the house, the relaxed atmosphere. They worried much less, she decided, about little things, they ate when they were hungry and did the laundry only when they were running out of clothes. They were, she decided, much less conscious of what other people thought of them than she was, but then again this was only two of them, she reminded herself. She also reminded herself that one of them at least appeared to have made living a life of carefree leisure an artform. In fact she pointed this out to Liam once, when they were at a midweek movie matinee, during intermission, when Sam, discovering Jane liked popcorn, had gone to get her some.

'Do you do this often?' she queried as they were left alone in the gloom of the theatre.

'As often as needs be,' Liam replied lazily.

Jane cast him a scornful look; she was in fact feeling scornful for more than one reason—the pretty young blonde usherette's state of utter confusion, even to dropping her torch upon laying eyes on Liam Benedict, had irked her considerably. In fact it had become increasingly obvious during their excursions that he had the same effect on most women.

'You are a hard man to pin down,' she said with irony. 'But do you think you should be corrupting Sam?'

'Well, Sam is on vacation and——'

'If he spends enough time with you he could consider going on permanent vacation,' she broke in vigorously, 'But you were going to say? And...?'

'Thank you for allowing me to finish,' he responded gravely, but although she couldn't read his expression in the gloom she knew he was laughing at her. 'I was about to remark that,' he paused, 'there could be some much more potent influences at work on Sam than I could bring to bear.'

'Oh? Such as?' Jane enquired coolly.

'I've changed my mind.'

Jane stared at him. 'What do you mean?'

'I'm no longer of a mind to comment on it, that's all. Here he is, by the way.'

Jane opened her mouth frustratedly but got no chance to pursue the matter further as Sam sat down beside her bearing not only popcorn but Coke and chocolates.

She did think of mentioning it again but discovered she was somewhat puzzled by Sam's relationship with Liam. There was almost a caring streak in Sam's attention to his cousin at times, she thought, and it was obvious he liked and admired Liam. Which led her to brood again on what a clever con Liam Benedict must be, but she just couldn't find it in her heart to try to disillusion Sam so she let the subject rest...

And somehow it became not only a carefree but comfortable week without her quite understanding how, and of her concerns, her major one dwindled and a new one sprang up.

For someone who had laid down the gauntlet as precisely as Liam Benedict had, he was behaving himself impeccably, but not only that—in friendliness and consideration. If it hadn't been for Sam, she might, she thought, have been better able to hold on to her suspicions that this was merely the lull before the storm. But, again, with Sam around it was curiously difficult to be suspicious of anything—he was such a honey, she decided. A charming mixture of eager boy with a terrific, infectious sense of humour, and serious young manhood. What didn't occur to her until towards the end of their week was that Sam believed himself to be falling in love with her. It should have. The way he washed her car for her and generally treated her like a fragile flower should have warned her. The open admiration in his eyes and the way he was happy to spend every moment in her company ought to have done the same, but all she really thought was that she'd like to have him as a brother, to tease gently and feed up. Then she asked him if he had a girlfriend and he replied very seriously that he preferred older women and he found girls his own age silly and immature.

Oh, no, Jane thought, seized at last with a dawning comprehension.

It was that evening while Sam was out that the matter came into the open, possibly because she was obviously preoccupied and tense.

Liam said suddenly, 'Penny for your thoughts, Jane?'

She focused her gaze on him slowly. 'I've got the horrible feeling your cousin is...is, well——'

'Completely bowled over and smitten by you? You're dead right,' he said with a grin.

Jane sprang up. 'But that's impossible!'

'It's not, you know, but he'll get over it. Just keep him at arm's length——'

'If you imagine I would do anything other,' Jane broke in crossly, 'I——'

'I don't now, but I wasn't sure whether you were aware of your effect on him.'

'I *wasn't*.' She stopped. 'Is *that* what you meant at the movies? Of all the——'

'Jane,' he interrupted patiently, 'let's not allow this to degenerate into one of our slanging matches. I thought we'd gone past all that.'

Jane took a few deep breaths and sat down but she said, although with restraint, 'You started it. You virtually accused me of leading him on.'

'What I meant was,' he paused, 'your degree of unawareness in certain matters is a little surprising.'

Jane said hastily, 'This was your idea, having Sam stay.'

'In other words, I got you into it, I should get you out of it?' His lips twisted. 'I promise you, what I recommended is all it needs. Unless you can come up with some competition?' He lifted an eyebrow at her.

'No, I can't! And that's the other strange thing,' she said rashly. 'In light of the things *you* once said to me...I mean...' She saw the trap too late and broke off.

'You mean how can I sit back and allow Sam to make any running with you? I don't regard him as serious competition, and anyway I'm biding my time.'

'I suspected as much, you know!'

'Did you? I hadn't lulled you into a false sense of security then? Good.'

'Liam——' she regarded him with a sudden frown '—why don't we forget all about it? I—to tell you the truth, I've really enjoyed this week. You've both been good company and,' she gestured ruefully, 'well, couldn't we just leave it there?'

He took his time about answering. 'In some ways I wish we could,' he said slowly at last. 'But I don't think it's possible.'

'Why?'

He shrugged and returned her regard wryly. 'You surely can't be *that* unaware, Jane?'

CHAPTER FOUR

JANE took a breath and tried to think of a way of covering her tracks at the same time as she wondered why she was still hiding behind the cover of 'experience' and wondered how 'unaware' she really was. To make matters worse, she suddenly wasn't all that unaware, she discovered, as the silence stretched. He might be a veritable thorn in her side but he was also incredibly attractive, she acknowledged with an inward tremor, and not only because of his magnificent physique, his good looks, but also because of the intelligence in his eyes—how could she have ever doubted it, even if he was wasting it? And because he could be *nice* and fun to be with. The thought that he found her desirable was...what? She glanced down at her long grey flannel skirt worn with a pearly angora sweater then looked up abruptly to see him watching her in a way that, although he was sprawled in his favourite chair, wasn't particularly lazy. In fact it transmitted a sort of electric impulse to her nerve-endings and made her feel that he was looking right through her clothes, making her feel extremely conscious of her body in a way she never had before. Added to this was the quite appallingly acute way she was suddenly conscious of his in a manner that was no different probably from what was experienced by every girl, usherettes included, who had ever beheld him with a little thrill of awe and wondered a bit dazedly what it would be like to be made love to by him.

'Jane?'

She banished her unbelievable fantasies with an effort and took refuge in an enigmatic shrug.

'Tell me something,' he said with a faint frown. 'You act as if...' He paused. 'As if you've never had any friendly male company—outside the context of career rivalry and men wanting to sleep with you.'

Jane grimaced at his uncanny perceptiveness but was relieved. 'Perhaps it's because I grew up in a household of women. My father left my mother quite early in the piece, and left her very bitter, incidentally.'

'You and your mother,' he said slowly, 'but not your sister, apparently?'

Jane grimaced. 'Well, Amanda was very young, but I sometimes wonder if he didn't leave her with a legacy of——' She spread her hands and shrugged.

'Tell me,' he invited.

'I don't know,' she frowned, 'but I've sometimes wondered if Amanda...if the way she is is a reaching out for the affection she missed out on.'

'Do you ever see him?'

'No. I—don't even know if he's alive,' she said sadly.

'Well, why don't you find out? Is your mother still alive?'

Jane blinked at him. 'No. You know I've never thought about doing that.' A sudden tremor of excitement ran through her and two seconds later a shiver of apprehension. 'Perhaps it's best to...'

'To let sleeping dogs lie? I wonder. He could hold the key to your personality.'

'Tell me why I'm such a freak,' she said with asperity.

'You said it,' he retorted. 'I don't happen to think you are at all. For what it's worth,' his eyes lingered on her, 'you've been fun to be with these past days, Jane.'

'When,' she said huskily, 'is the fun going to stop and the fight begin?'

'Why don't we have a preliminary skirmish right now?'

'What do you mean?' she whispered, her eyes widening.

'Did you ever kiss James?'

'No. What's that got to do with it?'

He eyed her dispassionately. 'Do you enjoy being kissed?'

She lifted her shoulders. 'I don't enjoy being sort of tested out on the subject. If that's what you had in mind.'

'Has anyone kissed you against your will out of sheer frustration?'

'Yes, once, as a matter of fact.' She looked faintly rueful.

'He was probably driven mad by your cool superiority,' Liam commented.

'I wasn't trying to be coolly superior, for your information,' she returned exasperatedly, 'or coolly anything.'

'It might come naturally to you, Jane,' he observed idly.

'I thought you just said you didn't believe I was a frigid freak?' she countered.

'I don't. Cool superiority is not quite the same thing. Besides which, some girls need to be coaxed into the art of kissing to appreciate its finer points.'

She strove for a casual approach. 'Well, of course there's an art to—any science?' she queried quizzically.

'Definitely. Chemistry, but a much more subtle and mysterious kind of chemistry than they teach you at school.'

Jane pursed her lips and lay back in her chair, pushing her hair off her neck. 'I'll give you this, Liam,' she said slowly. 'You're almost impossible to beat in an argument. I think *you* should have been a lawyer. But tell me something, tell me about *your* love-life.'

He considered and smiled fleetingly. 'You're obviously well versed in that old technique of attack being the best means of defence, Ms Mathieson, LL.B. What can I say to set your mind at rest? I'm thirty-two and I'm not inexperienced either. But I would strongly dispute any claims that I was any sort of a profligate Lothario.'

'Any affairs that lasted for some time?'

'I'm not into one-night stands if that's what you mean.' She thought he was looking at her with a glint of curiosity and wondered why.

She said, with some asperity, 'Yes, you really should have been a lawyer, talking of techniques and how to be evasive.' And then a look of confusion crossed her face. 'You know, some things about you just don't add up.'

'Which ones?'

'Well...' She hesitated and it struck her that despite his apparent lack of any career, any job even, it was getting harder to equate Liam Benedict with the drifter and layabout he was; he just didn't look like one for one thing, he didn't look dissipated, and although he certainly took things easy it wasn't in a slapdash, inherently lazy way—what was it? she wondered. 'Well...' she said, again uncertainly, because there was a part of her that still didn't want to give him credit for anything, she discovered. Then she heard a car, realised Sam was driving in—and took the easy way out. 'Forget all that—what am I going to do about Sam?' she demanded.

'Before we forget "all that" temporarily, may I say that I think you're quite unique, Jane? You're—to quote Sam—gorgeous, put together in a way that few men could resist, you have a brilliant mind and great ambition, yet you have style that reflects a subtle sensuality you don't seem to be altogether aware of, and you're fiery and cynical. That's quite a combination. What you're like in bed is quite mind-boggling.'

Jane muttered something wholly inaudible then said broodingly, 'I was quite right about you——'

'Which bit?'

'The bit about being sent here especially to torment the life out of me. The bit about—oh, what's the use? Just don't try to kiss me, Liam Benedict,' she said fiercely. 'I must warn you I'm liable to bite.'

'I had actually changed my mind about that. I'd already got those vibes. Anyway, there's Sam.'

'Sam!' Jane sat up exasperatedly.

'Just treat him as if you were an older sister. It won't last long.'

'I wouldn't mind having him for a brother,' Jane said slowly. 'The last thing I want to do is hurt his feelings.'

'How come you're so fond of Sam?' Liam asked quizzically. 'And before you raise your hackles and bare your teeth at me, I mean in a purely platonic way.'

Jane thought for a bit then looked surprised. 'I keep thinking how lucky his mother must be.'

Liam laughed outright. 'If you don't want to hurt his feelings, don't tell him that.'

'Tell who what?' Sam breezed in, glowing with vitality. 'I'm starving, by the way!'

'What's new?' his cousin and his other cousin's wife's sister chorused ruefully.

The next day was Sunday and one of those beautiful mid-winter days when the sky was clear, the sun shone and it was a penance to be inside.

'Let's go to St Helena!' Sam cast aside the Sunday papers impatiently. 'Your old boat could do with a spin, Liam, I'm sure!'

Liam looked up and grimaced. 'If it hasn't seized up from lack of use—like me,' he added obliquely.

Jane was washing the breakfast dishes and she looked across at him curiously.

'But it wouldn't—I mean,' Sam said, 'there's no problem for you going boating, is there?'

'None at all,' Liam replied with a crooked grin. 'Jane?'

Jane blinked then frowned. 'You mean—St Helena, the island in Moreton Bay?'

'The same,' Liam agreed. 'Ever been there?'

'I—er—have never been on a boat...'

'I don't believe it!' Sam stared at her incredulously. 'To live virtually *on* Moreton Bay, not to mention the Brisbane River—oh, Jane!' He bounded across to her and took the tea-towel out of her hands. 'Have we got a treat in store for you!'

'No, look,' she protested, 'you go. I don't happen to *like* boats and Moreton Bay can be——'

'How do you know if you've never been on one? And Moreton Bay is a piece of cake on a day like today. Besides which St Helena is only a hop, skip and a jump from Manly, where Liam keeps the boat, anyway!'

'I don't suppose it would be any good handcuffing myself to the nearest tree,' Jane observed gloomily a couple of hours later as she surveyed the forest of masts in the Manly boat harbour. 'What kind of a boat is this, and how come when you don't even have a car you can afford a boat?'

They were standing on the refuelling jetty. Sam had offered to retrieve the boat from where it was penned.

Liam looked down at her with his eyes amused. 'We won't let anything happen to you. You look the part if nothing else.' His gaze roamed over her slim figure clad in navy-blue trousers and a white jumper and rested briefly on the white bow tying back her hair. 'Relax,' he added.

'What if I get seasick?'

'You'll hardly have time—here he is.' He pointed.

Jane's eyes widened, for what Sam was approaching in was not some battered tin dinghy as she'd expected but a trim sleek little speedboat with a very powerful outboard even to the uninitiated eye. It also on closer inspection proved to have a beautifully upholstered interior with four comfortable seats beneath the sun canopy.

'Going like a charm,' Sam called as he nosed into the jetty. 'I spoke to the mechanic looking after her and he said he took her for a spin last week and everything's hunky dory. Welcome aboard, Jane!'

Jane hesitated, her confusion jostling with her reluctance. 'Did you win this from someone?' she said not quite beneath her breath, and, 'I'm surprised you haven't cashed it in.'

'Cashed it in?' Sam caught the last part and looked horrified. 'Why would he do that?'

'Jane is merely expressing her nerves in a roundabout way,' Liam murmured and climbed aboard then held out his hand to her. 'You'll be quite safe, Jane, I promise you.' His eyes caught hers and she wanted to say, 'Why should I believe you?' Yet she did—there was something rock-like and entirely dependable about Liam Benedict at that moment and she couldn't for the life of her understand why...

'Well...' She put her hand in his, her new confusion showing quite plainly, and it was that that made her keep both feet on the jetty.

He smiled faintly, released her hand—but to put both his round her waist—and he swung her on board effortlessly. The boat rocked and he put his arms around her then, steadying her, and for one unbelievable moment she closed her eyes and rested against him and wished she didn't have to leave the reassuring sanctuary of his arms. When this dawned on her she went still and raised her head slowly. He was looking down at her expressionlessly, watching the slow colour rise beneath her skin and the way her eyes widened. But she couldn't tear them away and it was as if every line of his face, the blue of his eyes and the thick darkness of his hair, the strength of his neck and shoulders beneath a grey tracksuit top today, were being engraved on her heart.

She closed her eyes and thought, No, this can't be happening to me if it's what I think it is—how does he do it? How humiliating...

It was Sam who saved her. 'Sit here, Jane. Can I drive, Liam? Are you comfortable, Jane? Oh, boy, what a day!'

Liam laughed and sat down behind them. 'Just take it gently, Sam,' he warned, however.

'As if I wouldn't,' Sam retorted with a pained look.

It was quite a day.

St Helena, formerly a penal settlement with some of its historic buildings still standing although crumbling, was set like a jewel in the pale blue, satin-smooth waters of Moreton Bay and after a sedate trip from Manly they went ashore and strolled through the ruins over the lush grass, drinking in the timeless feeling of the island. Then they walked back to the picnic area near the jetty and had their lunch beneath a huge, shady tree—a bought chicken and ham and a salad Jane had made hastily, and a bottle of Riesling.

'I have to say,' she wiped her fingers and took a sip of wine, 'that I've enjoyed this more than I'd have thought possible. I gather——' she waved to where the boat was tied along the jetty '—that that boat can go much faster but you didn't want to scare the life out of me. Thanks. And for everything else.'

'It can,' Sam said enthusiastically. 'Does that mean I can open her up going back?'

A look of wariness came to her eyes despite herself and her new mood and Liam grinned and said immediately. 'No, old son, I don't think that's what Jane meant. Why don't you give the boat a burn now—while your olders and betters relax a bit longer—get it out of your system?'

'What a brilliant idea! Can I really?'

Jane had to smile as she watched him bound away. Then she turned to Liam. 'You're very lucky, you know.'

He was lying stretched out on the blanket with his head propped on his hand while she was leaning back against the tree trunk.

'I am?' he murmured.

'Yes. You have a very nice family.' She stopped then looked straight into his eyes. 'But there are some things you're going to have to explain to me.'

'Such as?'

'How you can do this to them . . .'

He considered idly then said, 'Why are you concerning yourself so much with it, Jane?'

'It seems—it seems such an awful waste,' she said with a frustrated gesture.

'Does it also colour *your* view of me?' he suggested after a silent couple of minutes and when she'd thought he wasn't going to answer.

She plucked a stalk of grass and wondered why she felt oddly agitated. 'In what way?' she said at last.

He smiled faintly. 'I'm asking you. But let's try this for size. Would you be more amenable to my—er—attentions if you thought I was a respectable accountant or whatever?'

'Not at all,' Jane said stiffly. 'That has nothing to do with it...' But even as she spoke she couldn't help wondering a little wildly if it did.

'Good,' he murmured. 'Then we might be making a bit of progress.'

Jane's eyes widened. 'I didn't mean *that*!'

He sat up. 'What did you mean—on the boat?'

Their gazes locked and a pulse started to beat at the base of her throat and her cheeks reddened. 'I...' She licked her lips. 'Well, I think I can be forgiven anything I did then,' she said and winced at the air of desperation that came through, hoping she'd imagined it. 'I mean, you saw how scared I was of boats.'

'So that was all it was?'

It occurred to her later that she forgot to answer, so preoccupied was she with the deadly little battle raging within to do with an innate disability, it seemed, to lie, or to go on lying. But what is the truth? she wondered. That I'm like every other female who crosses his path, taken in by his looks, his physique? Surely not!

'Jane?'

Her eyes focused on him but she couldn't formulate any words.

And a look she couldn't quite decipher flickered across his eyes, part wry, part something else. Then he said,

'Your ribbon's coming undone. We're about,' he added, 'to be invaded by a boatload of tourists.'

She put a hand to her hair and twisted her head to look round the tree towards the jetty where a large cruise boat was tying up. 'Oh.' She pulled the ribbon off, put it between her teeth, combed her hair back with her fingers and retied it. 'What a pity,' she said lamely and rested her hands in her lap.

'Never mind,' he drawled, and this time it was impossible to misunderstand the look of irony in his eyes. 'Sam's got tired of burning up the waterways, so we might as well go home.'

That night, she decided to go back to work the next morning.

She caused a minor sensation when she appeared at breakfast dressed for work. Not with Liam—he merely glanced at her and glanced away as if it was only what he'd expected. Sam, on the other hand, stared at her open-mouthed.

She wore a slim, elegant charcoal suit with a yellow silk blouse and black leather accessories. Her hair was gathered back in a neat chignon, her make-up perfect in every detail and her expression withdrawn and preoccupied.

It was not quite the jolly breakfast they'd become accustomed to as she declined an omelette bursting with tomato and mushrooms in favour of cereal and fruit. In fact this choice provoked a rather deadly little debate.

'You're not afraid of putting on weight, are you?' Liam queried.

In view of the discovery that she no longer had to pin up her skirts, Jane was forced to make a fairly truthful if oblique reply. 'I'm back to normal now.'

He regarded her meditatively. 'You still look as if a good puff of wind would blow you away.'

'That's nonsense—besides,' she retorted unwisely, 'you're only talking from a preference for well-built Amazonian types.'

He didn't say anything, just held her gaze captive in an exercise of mysterious power that not only annoyed her but also troubled her and made her feel hot and foolish, especially as she recalled the things he'd once detailed that he found physically appealing about her.

She twitched her gaze away angrily at last. 'As a matter of fact this is a much healthier breakfast,' she said with a return of spirit.

'For a mouse,' he agreed.

'Haven't you ever heard of cholesterol?'

'Oh, yes. I was referring to the size of it and I doubt if a small portion of this omelette as well would do you any harm. It's been made with fresh farm eggs, fresh milk, et cetera, and in a non-stick skillet, and it might just give you the energy to keep abreast of others without having to paddle so hard.'

'There is,' Jane said with difficulty, 'no need for you to concern yourself about that.'

'There's every need, Jane.'

Again blue eyes clashed with green but Sam came to the rescue, or tried to. 'He's right, you know. My mum reckons a good breakfast is essential.'

Jane glanced at her watch and said with sudden, furious exasperation, 'All right! I'll eat it, but only because I'm running late now and I don't have the time to argue with you two.'

Liam dished her up a small portion and said tranquilly, 'Remind me to show you some anti-stress exercises, Jane. They could help you too.'

Jane took a deep breath and said sweetly, 'Removing yourself from my presence this early in the morning would be a big help.' She ate steadily for a few minutes. Then she touched a napkin to her lips and stood up. 'I'm off. Have a good day, gentlemen!'

But Liam chose to escort her down to her car, to make sure, he said, that it started.

'Of course it's going to start,' she said crossly, going down the back steps carefully in her heels. 'Ever since you fixed it, it's started first time!'

'Why are you in such a state, Jane?' he asked, as they walked into the garage.

Jane took another deep breath and turned to him. 'If you really want to know,' she regarded him with the kind of look she normally reserved for things that crawled out from under rocks, 'I was trying to distance myself from Sam this morning, but *you* reduced me to the status of a recalcitrant schoolgirl and you both ended up patronising me in a manner——'

'Don't work yourself up any more, Jane,' he broke in to advise and added, 'Perhaps you are more of a recalcitrant schoolgirl than you realise and that's why this polished image of a mature lady lawyer doesn't quite sit.'

'Oh!'

'Or perhaps,' he leant his shoulders against the wall, 'you're running scared. Because of what happened yesterday. I wasn't going to mention it but if it's upsetting you to this degree I think we should have it out, don't you?'

Jane stared at him then she turned away jerkily and fumbled in her bag for her car keys. He waited until she got them in the door and was about to pull it open, then he put his hand over hers and stopped her. 'Jane?'

It was said coolly but with an undercurrent of something impatient and sardonic.

'Let me go,' she whispered.

'Not until you tell me the truth.'

She twisted her wrist but it was useless. 'Liam—you can't do this to me,' she said. 'I'm going to be late for work. Why *now* ... ?' She stopped and grimaced at the pleading note she'd heard in her voice.

He let her hand go but turned her to face him. 'Because I'm interested, that's why,' he said wryly and scanned her face and her deeply troubled expression. 'Don't look like that,' he went on barely audibly with a faint smile twisting his lips. 'It's not the end of the world. If I affect you, you do the same to me. I've told you that. Surely we know each other well enough now to be honest—in fact I can tell you honestly what I feel right now. I'd like very much to kiss you goodbye and I'd like to think it would give you a sense of warmth and encouragement. That's what the best of relationships are supposed to be about, aren't they?'

For a long moment Jane stared up at him transfixed again, her lips parted, and something in her eyes that was part stunned, partly a dawning sort of curiosity. Then she blinked abruptly and tried to turn away but before she could do anything he put one arm around her waist, bent her backwards at the same time as he held her body into his in the kind of embrace that was all-powerful and left her in no doubt that she was about to be kissed deliberately and provocatively and there was not a thing she could do about it.

There wasn't. Not that she responded, she was too stunned for that, but the kind of outrage she should have experienced was oddly tempered when it was over, when he lifted his head and his eyes laughed at her although his expression was grave and innocent.

She did stumble as if her knees were suddenly weaker than normal, and he steadied her then even had the gall to settle the collar of her blouse and smooth her jacket.

She did whisper, 'How dare you?' but not with much ferocity, as he inspected her face keenly.

But he only replied, 'Your lipstick needs a bit of attention, otherwise you're—perfect.'

She tried to gather herself. 'If that's what you meant by encouragement——'

'It wasn't. That was a purely chauvinistic impulse of the basest kind—I admit it,' he drawled, then his lips quirked. 'That doesn't mean the other kind of reassurance and encouragement doesn't exist but——'

But Jane clenched her hands into fists, glared at him as if she'd like very much to take a swipe at him then said with a toss of her head, 'I am going to *work*, Mr Benedict. You may stay here and theorise until the cows come home for all I care—just get out of my way!'

'Certainly,' he replied readily and opened the car door for her. 'I'd hate to get beaten up this early in the day.'

'Oh!' Jane ground her teeth and virtually leapt into the car before her frustrations overcame her.

'Have a good day, ma'am,' he said, not without a touch of irony, and closed the door gently.

It was mid-afternoon before Laura got the chance to comment because of the cracking pace Jane had set to clear the backlog of work on her desk. But by then Jane herself ran out of energy and her secretary surprised her sitting motionless at her desk, staring into space.

'What's wrong?' she demanded.

'I probably didn't have enough omelette,' Jane said gloomily.

Laura dumped a pile of letters on the desk and sank into a chair. 'What's that supposed to mean?'

Jane sighed and flexed her shoulders. 'Nothing.'

'So tell me.'

'Tell you what?'

Laura got up and closed the door. 'What it's like living with a gorgeous man like Liam Benedict, darling,' she said. 'In a purely platonic sense, of course.'

Jane grimaced. 'His cousin has joined us.'

'Do you mean to tell me you're now living with *two* gorgeous hunks—I presume if they're cousins there's a resemblance.'

Jane raised an eyebrow. 'That's the kind of presumption one should never make in law. In fact Liam Benedict has a brother——'

'Married to your sister.'

'Married to my sister,' Jane agreed, 'who bears little resemblance to him at all.'

'Is the cousin then a weedy intellectual?' Laura enquired.

'He's not. He's like a younger pea in a pod——'

'Well!'

Jane rubbed her brow. 'How did we get on to this?'

'You don't want to talk about him, do you?' Laura said shrewdly. 'That's not a good sign, Jane. You know I really thought you looked a lot better when you arrived this morning.'

'That wouldn't have been hard considering how I looked the last time you saw me.'

'I meant, from how you looked *before* you—er—ran into Liam Benedict.'

'Yes, well,' Jane started to leaf through the letters, 'they're fattening me up. Is this all the dictation?'

Laura looked at her piercingly, then she nodded. 'You're not going to give me any more, are you?' she queried plaintively. 'I've typed my fingers to the bone.'

'No. Thanks,' Jane said listlessly.

Laura sat back with a relieved sigh. 'A friend of mine used to work for him, by the way.'

'Work for who?'

'Your new housemate, darling, but before you jump to the conclusion that I was discussing *you in any way*,' Laura said hastily, 'I merely happened to mention to *her* that I'd met this absolutely divine man—all too briefly, alas.' She grimaced.

Jane stopped shuffling through Laura's letters. 'Worked for Liam? What doing?'

'Secretarial—well, she worked for the firm but——'

'When was this?'

Laura frowned. 'About a year ago—Jane, you look a little strange. Are you sure you should have come back so soon?'

'What *firm*?' Jane said tautly.

'His own. Benedict & Benedict, stockbrokers. Haven't you heard of them? But as I was about to say, she assured me every girl who worked there was wildly in love with him—to no avail at all,' Laura finished sadly. 'Jane——'

'I don't believe it!' Jane said through her teeth.

'Oh, it's true. I mean you've just got to look at him to fall for him——'

'Not *that*!' Jane ground out.

Laura looked startled. 'What, then?'

Jane glared at her then she closed her eyes frustratedly. 'Just go away, please, Laura,' she said wearily.

CHAPTER FIVE

LIAM was alone when Jane got home but he was setting the table for three so she gathered that Sam wasn't far away. And she compressed her lips and swept into her bedroom to change without a word to his mild look of enquiry.

'I gather,' he said when she emerged; he was sitting down reading the evening paper, looking totally relaxed, 'I'm still in disgrace.'

She drew an angry breath but steeled herself. 'No. No, you're not—but if you expect *me* to feel that way you may think again!'

'I don't,' he murmured with a laughing look, but then, as she put her hands on her hips and regarded him with magnificent scorn, his eyes narrowed. 'Are we talking about the same thing, though?'

'Probably not. I'm talking about a very successful stockbroking firm called Benedict & Benedict in which you happen to be the senior partner and in which you *worked* apparently until a couple of months ago!'

'Ah.' He laid the paper aside with a wry look. 'I didn't think I could keep it up for ever.'

'Are you talking about the...' she sought for words '...lying hoax, the deceitful game you've been playing with me since the day we met? Is that what you mean?' she demanded.

'Jane, sit down, don't work yourself up any more,' he advised. 'Let me get you a drink; you look as if you could use it.'

She made a wholly unintelligible, exasperated sound, and, because she was possessed of a desire to hit him again, sank into a chair instead.

He went about getting their drinks silently and handed her hers without a word before sitting down opposite her. 'I must admit,' he said finally, 'that your sweeping assumptions about me activated my—er—baser instincts and prompted me to maintain the charade.'

'My sweeping assumptions!' she marvelled. 'Your own brother told me...' She stopped abruptly. 'Well, he did,' she went on but much less forcefully.

'Look, I've got a fair idea how that came about. James was rather annoyed with me. I—had a bit of a car accident and I had to take some time off work. He wanted me to stay here so he could keep an eye on me but I didn't really want to,' he shrugged, 'impose on anyone, so I decided to go to New Zealand for an extended holiday. I think he was a little bit piqued,' he said wryly.

Jane stared at him and remembered James's words: 'He's a hard man to pin down...doing heaven knows what, but he has plenty of friends over there so he should survive.' Her eyes widened and she swallowed suddenly. 'What...' She cleared her throat. 'What about the house, though? I got the distinct impression——' She broke off and bit her lip.

Liam grinned. 'Perhaps I did lead you on there but in fact the reason I persuaded James to hang on to the house for the time being is because this suburb is steadily becoming more fashionable, these old suburbs close to town are, and I think if we wait we can get more money for it. He was a bit annoyed with me about that too but I'd be very surprised if I'm proved wrong.'

Jane digested it all and started to go a bright, mortified red. Then as he watched her steadily, she licked her lips and said, 'My apologies, but—well, you *did* lead me on,' she said intensely.

'I'm afraid I just couldn't resist it.'

'Oh!' Jane took a large swallow of her drink, which went down the wrong way, and when her fit of spluttering subsided she discovered she was feeling even more hard done by. 'How you must have laughed at me!'

'A bit,' he conceded.

'Well, if I'm supposed to feel in any way chastened, I don't,' she said moodily. 'I may have made some...assumptions, but...what about Sam?'

'What about him?'

'Is he in on this too?'

'I asked him not to mention the accident, that's all.'

'So that's why——' She stood up abruptly. 'It must have been a pretty bad accident!'

He grimaced and shrugged.

Jane stared at him frustratedly, her feelings in an absolute turmoil, which took the form of an utterance even she couldn't help feeling guilty about but couldn't seem to help all the same. She said, 'I feel really dreadful now, thanks to you!'

'You don't have to—and you didn't a few moments ago,' he pointed out.

'Of course I did,' she said scathingly. 'I just didn't want to admit it. How would *you* feel in my place?'

'I think,' he said slowly, 'I'd be a bit wary of prejudging people in future.'

Jane's nostrils flared but there was enough truth in it to add to her guilt. 'You're right,' she said with sudden decision. 'I will. But I still feel you don't come out of it entirely smelling of roses either.'

'Oh, I quite agree with you.' He looked at her gravely.

'Yes, well, if you think I'm taken in by that,' she muttered, 'I'm not——'

'Jane, would it help to speculate on what drew *both* of us into this—situation?'

'What do you mean?' She eyed him suspiciously.

'I'm talking about the effect we have on each other that appears to have led us into some rash judgements and actions.'

He said it quietly and dispassionately but it had the curious effect, talking of that kind of thing, she mused a little bitterly, of causing her mind to take wings, in a manner of speaking, back to how she'd felt this morning and how she'd felt yesterday in his arms. She took a breath and looked away.

'I don't think it would help much, no,' she said.

'You still refuse to acknowledge it, in other words?'

She tried to resist looking at him; she sipped her drink and placed it carefully on the table, but in the end it was useless. She looked into his eyes at last and said baldly, 'Yes.'

'Why?'

'I'd prefer not to go into it—well, no, I will. I'm not easy prey, Liam, I never have been. I know,' she gestured as he went to speak, 'you're going to deny it but I resent being...sort of tested out under false premises, which I think your charade was mostly in aid of; I *resent*—even while I feel guilty about making the kind of snap judgements I did—the whole nature of this, your original challenge, everything to do with it. I'm sorry but I can't help it and a slight, fleeting curiosity about a good-looking man who has women lining up for his *attentions*, apparently, can never overcome the rest of it.' She stared at him with her eyes shadowed but defiant.

'Bravo, Jane,' he said softly. 'You know, you're an even more worthy opponent than I thought.'

Her eyes widened then she frowned. 'If by that you mean what I think you mean——'

'That it's still on? It is for me, Jane.' His lips twisted. 'It is for me. There's Sam, by the way. Aren't we lucky how he always manages to defuse things?'

It was an uneasy evening despite Sam's powers of defusing things and not helped for Jane by Sam's revelations when something prompted her to ask him about Liam's accident.

'Oh, so you know now,' he said approvingly. 'I guess I can understand Liam not wanting people to go on about it but you are family, aren't you?' He smiled at her engagingly. 'Well, not related, thankfully, but family of a kind. He was lucky to survive, in fact we thought we'd lost him,' he added seriously. 'You should have seen the car—the other party was completely in the wrong.'

'But he's fine now?' Jane queried.

'They think so, but he was a wreck for a while. Everyone was furious with him for insisting on recuperating in New Zealand but he's even talking about going back to work. He still has a problem with one knee, though. They're hoping it doesn't need an operation and so far it looks good.'

Jane took all this to bed with her and tried very hard to still the curious little pang of pain she felt at the thought of Liam Benedict being a wreck. Remember how he conned you instead, she advised herself; remember his challenge...

She was still giving herself this advice when she came home one evening to find herself alone and a note on the fridge to the effect that both Sam and Liam would be out until late—together with the admonition to lock herself in.

She breathed a sigh of relief and did just that. Then she set about having a long pleasurable evening on her own. She had a light meal and did some chores such as sorting through her clothes and deciding what needed dry-cleaning, made some running repairs and polished her shoes and handbags. Then she washed her hair, wound it in a towel and sat down in front of the television wearing only a warm woollen robe the colour of rose quartz, and briefs, to do her nails. But she opened the bottle then found herself staring at it and wondering why her pleasant evening was not being as enjoyable as she'd hoped, why she felt restless—and lonely? That was when, although it was only eight-thirty, Liam came in.

He threw a set of car keys on the kitchen table and raised a quizzical eyebrow. Until now she had strictly pursued all such feminine occupations in the privacy of her bedroom and the bathroom.

She stared at him frustratedly with the nail-polish brush held in mid-air for a moment then said severely, 'I wasn't expecting you. *Yet.*'

'So I see,' he murmured. 'I've bought myself a car, by the way, and I went to see some friends who were on their way out. But is there a problem?' He strolled through into the lounge, pulled off his reefer jacket, slung it over a chair and immediately filled the room with an aura of vitality of the sheer masculine variety, plus she just knew he was secretly laughing at her and she felt her cheeks redden, to her annoyance.

'Of course there's a problem,' she snapped and screwed the lid on to the nail-polish. 'Do you think I go around inviting an audience when I do this kind of thing?'

He sat down on cushioned stool about a foot away from her and picked up the colourful little bottle she'd just manhandled shut and turned it over in his hand thoughtfully. 'No, but it's not as if you've been caught doing something shocking. I have seen women wash their hair and paint their nails before, I don't think there's anything immoral in it. It can be—quite charming.' He looked at her with a wicked little glint in his eye.

Jane tightened her mouth. 'Women you were sleeping with,' she said frostily. 'Not—virtual strangers.' She knew as soon as she said it that it sounded ridiculous not only because they were hardly strangers any more but also because it sounded incredibly prudish. But then again, she felt, she discovered, as her hand wandered to the V of her robe and closed it up to her throat, if not prudish, certainly a bit shy; it was curiously disconcerting to be caught out like this with but one stitch of underwear on into the bargain.

His gaze followed the movement of her hand, lingering on the way she clenched it around the rose wool, drifted down to her legs, which were bare from the knees down then came back to her face as she visibly restrained herself from smoothing her robe which was already modestly closed over her lap. It was as if, she thought irritably, she was determined to make him *aware* that she had hardly anything beneath the robe.

'That's true,' he said idly.

She frowned. 'What's true?'

'It's generally women you sleep with you see doing this—it *can* be something quite intimate. It still doesn't make it anything immodest, particularly as we happen

to share a house. So far as sleeping with each other
goes——'

'Don't,' Jane said hastily.

'Don't what?' he queried innocently.

She bit her lip. 'Don't *speculate* as if it's all a game,
a sort of seduction stakes...' She broke off frustratedly.

'Actually,' he turned the bottle over then put it down
gently and raised his eyes to hers, 'I too had the feeling
things had gone beyond a game, and when I say that I
mean——' he paused and eyed her gravely '—that despite your protestations it's quite a serious consideration
with you now. Us sleeping together,' he added for absolute clarification. 'But being you, a first-class fighter,'
his lips twisted, 'there are certain inherent difficulties
about laying down your arms.' He smiled wryly.

Jane sprang up, tightening her sash viciously and
caught the towel as it came tumbling down, then threw
it away and ran her fingers through her damp hair. 'You
thought wrong,' she said grimly. 'I haven't laid down
any arms, because I don't want to. If you really believe
I'm in any hurry to add myself to the long list of women
you've been *intimate* with, you're——'

She stopped abruptly as he got up, picked up the towel
and laid it over a chair then came towards her. 'Liam...'
The words got stuck in her throat.

He stopped in front of her, so close that she had to
tilt her head to look up at him, and she thought he was
perfectly serious for once as he said, 'I would disagree
about it being such a long list, but you know, Jane, there
are some women who *never* know how to lay down their
arms and it's often partly because they have this secret
desire to be overpowered. Is that your problem? I'd be
quite happy to oblige, assuming you could be honest
about it.'

Her lips parted and her eyes widened in shock. 'No,' she said hoarsely. 'Oh, no——'

'Then why this extreme reluctance to admit that a few days ago when your guard was down——?'

'Because it *was* down,' she whispered. 'I mean I——'

'You mean you liked it,' he said drily. 'You would like it even more now, you know. So would I, let's be honest. I should imagine that, beneath that robe you're wearing like a suit of armour because you haven't got anything on underneath it, your skin is fresh and like ivory satin; your hair certainly smells wonderful.' He wound some round his hand and watched the way it held the curl when he let it go. 'And you were relaxed.' His gaze caught hers again. 'You'd done all the little things girls like to do—what better time to let a lover slide his hands over your body and be really intimate with you?'

It all flashed through Jane's mind, every last little intimate nuance, so that her fresh ivory skin grew warm and flushed beneath the robe and her mind registered how lonely and restless she'd felt until he'd come home...

She looked away and said with a nuance of her own—slight despair which she prayed he didn't catch, 'I'm going to bed.'

He made no move to detain her.

It was in the darkness and privacy of her bedroom that she thought of all the *right* things to say...

'Yes, Mr Benedict, that's all very well, but on your past record I've got the feeling we're looking for two different things....'

She broke off her monologue with herself and winced. What am I looking for? she wondered, and added a little sadly to herself, I wasn't looking for anything until Liam

Benedict sprang into my life. And the plain miserable fact of it is that I'm now fighting tooth and nail to...not to be affected by him this way, not to be like every other girl who is suddenly lonely and discontented with the little chores she used to enjoy doing—how well he knows us, she marvelled, damn him! And not to be curious and be unable to help picturing him making love to me, picturing what it would be like to be really close to him and whether I could draw encouragement and succour from a relationship with him, perhaps give it?

'Wonder if I'm in love.' She closed her eyes but couldn't stop her heartbeat from accelerating or her mind's eye from picturing his hands slipping beneath her robe, perhaps while she was lying in his arms on the settee...

Several days passed during which they didn't have a lot to do with each other, mainly because Jane kept herself scrupulously to herself whenever they did happen to be at home together, which was only in the evenings anyway. This didn't go unnoticed by Sam, who wore a puzzled frown occasionally, and she couldn't help regretting the loss of their easy camaraderie, but how could you be comradely and easy with a man who alternately made you so aware of him and accused you of not being able to put down your arms because of a secret desire to be overpowered? Yes, remember that one, she advised herself, and what a monumental ego it represents.

It also didn't help to see Liam Benedict getting back into the swing of things or realising that a lot of people hadn't known he was back in Brisbane, a lot of people who seemed to like him a lot, and among them some very elegant, glamorous girls who hung on his every word. It was when she started to speculate on how he'd managed to evade marriage for so long that she gave herself a severe talking to.

But one afternoon she got out of court earlier than expected yet too late to achieve much at the office so she went home to find a scenario that rather dispelled the image of a callow egotist she was trying so hard to build up in her mind.

She'd been leafing through the mail as she walked up the back steps but raised her head at an unexpected sound, then hurried in with a worried frown. And, to her extreme surprise, over the kitchen counter she saw a heavily pregnant woman reclining on the settee, three small children squashed together in an armchair looking apprehensive—and Liam putting the phone down on the counter.

'What...?'

'Ah, Jane,' he said easily. 'You couldn't have timed it better. Let me introduce you. This is Mary Jones. She was waiting for a bus at the bus stop down the road when she found herself unexpectedly going into labour.'

'*Labour*...?'

'Mmm.' His tone didn't change but he reached across and put his hand over hers, a firm grip, and stared into her eyes with a brief look that said quite clearly, 'Now don't *you* panic...'

Mary Jones raised her head and there was sweat rolling off her brow as she said with an effort, 'I'm not due for another three weeks—oh, thank heavens you were driving down the road, Mr Benedict!' She took a breath. 'The children?'

'They're fine,' Liam said soothingly. 'Jane, why don't you give them a soft drink?' He crossed the room and sat down beside the pregnant woman and took her hand. 'The ambulance will be here in a tick and your husband's firm is paging him. They're going to tell him to go straight to the hospital. Jane?'

Jane blinked then was galvanised into action. 'Of course. Here we go, kids. Let's see, how about some Coke and I've got some biscuits; why don't you come and choose your favourites?'

They came, still looking nervous, then relieved when there were no further heartfelt groans from their mother as Liam sat beside her, holding her hand and talking to her quietly.

And indeed the ambulance did arrive shortly but when Jane suggested the children stay with her they started to cry and Mary Jones suddenly looked up at Liam with fear in her eyes and seemed reluctant to let go of his hand, so the ambulance officer said cheerfully, 'I reckon you all ought to come! It's not far and we ought to make it in plenty of time, and if their daddy's at the hospital they'll be fine.'

Which was how Jane came to take a trip to the Royal Women's one sunny winter's afternoon in an ambulance. I don't believe this, she thought to herself once, and amended it as she watched Mary Jones, who was even laughing a little now; I don't believe how a woman about to give birth can be so reassured by a perfectly strange man like this. How does he have this effect on everyone? And if he can do it for a stranger, what could he do if it were his child you were having?

'We'll have to take a taxi home. Hell!' Liam said some time later. 'At one stage I really thought I might have to deliver that baby myself. Thanks for the help.'

Jane shrugged. 'I didn't do much.' Barry Jones had arrived not long after they had to take charge of his family and had been as much taken with his wife's saviour as she had.

But, once in the taxi, Liam directed it not home but to a restaurant.

'Look...' Jane began.

'Not hungry?' he queried with a lifted eyebrow.

'Yes, I am,' she said unwisely, 'but——'

'They make a marvellous Moreton Bay bug dish here. Didn't you tell me once that you loved bugs?'

'Yes, I *did*, but——'

'I don't see the problem, then,' he drawled.

'You never *do*,' she retorted.

'Why don't you enlighten me, Jane?'

She breathed heavily. 'You should have asked first! I might have had something on——'

'Have you?'

'No! But——'

'Then will you have dinner with me, Jane, dear?' he murmured. 'I didn't think you'd feel like cooking after that ordeal. I know I don't.'

There was a chuckle from the front seat. 'Have it with him, lady,' the taxi driver advised.

Jane ground her teeth and relapsed into stony silence.

The restaurant was homely but dim and comfortable. Liam was obviously a cherished regular, which made for them getting the best table and considerable attention and caused Jane to say broodingly when they were alone at last, 'Do you charm *everyone*?'

Liam sat back and considered. 'You don't think a woman caught about to have a baby unexpectedly deserves to be charmed a little?'

Jane grimaced. 'Undoubtedly. It's everyone else that— oh, forget it.'

'Whatever you say,' he obliged, but his eyes were amused.

Jane coloured, sipped her drink and didn't reply.

'How was your day?' he asked after a while.

She shrugged. 'My client took exception to the barrister and wanted to change horses mid-stream, so to speak. We had to ask for an adjournment and were lucky to get it.' She moved her shoulders wearily then smiled faintly. 'She's a woman, the barrister; he's a very macho male as well as being a farmer with absolutely no understanding of the mechanics of the law and at one stage I thought they were going to come to blows. Women don't figure very high in his estimation at the moment. His wife, who persuaded him to retain this barrister in the first place, left him yesterday.'

'They say it never rains but it pours.'

'Mmm,' Jane agreed. 'I feel a bit sorry for him.'

Liam raised an eyebrow. 'Despite his anti-feminist sentiments?'

She laughed. 'Yes. You can have an incredible run of outs whatever your sentiments are and he certainly is at the moment.'

Their entrées arrived at that point, onion soup with crusty croutons floating on top and somehow, she wasn't sure how, Jane found herself relaxing, and they talked about nothing very serious but companionably. He chose a smooth white wine to go with their bugs, which arrived in their shells on a bed of fluffy white rice and Jane stared down at them, inhaled the delicate aroma of the sauce and sighed with appreciation.

Liam grinned. 'What would life be like without Moreton Bay bugs?' he murmured.

'I suppose you could always fall back on crayfish or lobster, but their flavour isn't quite so... sweet, is it?'

'Have you ever wanted to travel, Jane?'

'Oh, yes,' she said enthusiastically. 'But funnily enough it's the one thing I don't relish doing alone.' She stopped rather abruptly.

'Who did you envisage doing it with?'

She raised her green eyes to his and they were oddly confused.

'Not James?' he said with irony after a moment.

'Not—no,' she said with an effort. 'Someone who knew their way around, who knew where to find the true heart of places not just the touristy ones, someone you felt safe with and in——' She stopped again and bit her lip.

'In love with? In the manner James and Amanda are doing it at the moment, in other words?'

Jane transferred her attention back to her bugs. 'Yes—I cannot tell a lie,' she murmured with a sigh, but added with more spirit, 'I really don't know if James knows his way around the world any more than Amanda does.'

'I do.'

'I'm sure you do,' Jane replied tartly. 'Is there anything you don't know or can't do? Incidentally, I have to say I hope you don't actually trade on a set of genes that seems to make you irresistible to women—that would be wicked, you know.'

He merely eyed her narrowly for a brief moment then went on eating.

'What's *that* supposed to mean?' Jane demanded in a goaded sort of way.

He put down his fork, pushed his platter away and sat back with his wine. 'That I knew you'd have to relieve yourself of that sentiment before the evening was out, but, be that as it may, I can think of lots of out-of-the-way places you would love, some of them warm and tropical, where you wouldn't need to wear much more than a sarong and a bikini and a flower in your hair, some of them cold and crisp where you'd need to bundle up—all of them wonderful places to make love to you. Making love in foreign places is quite something. Cheers.' He raised his glass to her. 'So you were on the right track in your dreams, dear Jane,' he added quizzically as she started to blush.

'As a matter of interest,' he went on when she said nothing but ate with a great deal of determination, 'how *do* you like it?'

'Like what?' she said indistinctly through a mouthful of rice.

'Like to be made love to?'

She put her fork down, chewed her rice to the last grain, dabbed her lips with the napkin then leant her elbows on the table and clasped her hands thoughtfully—what she hoped would project an image of thoughtfulness, anyway. 'Are there so many different ways?'

His eyes laughed at her. 'Oh, there are. Some girls like to *be* undressed for example, some like to do it themselves, quite slowly and erotically—I think if I were making love to you, Jane, I'd like you to do it. There would have to be, forgive me,' his lips twisted rather wryly, 'but there would regrettably have to be a sense of triumph in that.'

Jane's fingers clenched together but she forced herself to say coolly, 'I can imagine.'

His eyes probed hers, and said drily and suddenly seriously, 'I wonder. There's also nothing wrong in giving yourself honestly and in joy to a man.'

She caught her breath and was unable to tear her gaze away, but fortunately the proprietor chose that moment to come up to the table and ask how their meals had been.

And the evening seemed to go downhill after that. They left not long afterwards and were quite silent in the taxi home.

To her relief Sam was home and bearer of some news.

'Got a call for you, Liam, but it was a bit hard to make head or tail of it. Some really excited guy rang to say the baby was a boy, they were both fine, they'd decided to call it after you and wondered if you'd be a godfather to it. But he forgot to tell me who he was.'

Liam laughed and filled him in.

But Jane took herself to bed rather abruptly, thereby causing Sam to look disappointed and wistful and Liam merely to wish her goodnight lazily but with a mocking little glint in his eyes.

She leant back against her bedroom door breathing raggedly and prayed for some composure. Then she wondered dully how many more times she would have to flee to bed to get away from Liam Benedict and what he did to her without even laying a hand on her.

I've got to be objective about this, she thought, and pushed herself away from the door. I've got to admit I am attracted to him—and fascinated and intrigued—but how can I help also being very wary and wondering just how *serious* he is?

She opened her wardrobe door and stared at herself in the mirror, then she turned away with a sigh because what she'd been seeing was not Jane Mathieson LL.B dressed in tailored suit but a girl in a sarong with a flower in her hair and—love in her eyes.

*   *   *

She was still thinking along those lines as she drove home through the early gloom of a winter's evening the next day.

But when she arrived once again the lounge, visible through the kitchen, was unusually populated, but this time with policemen including Liam's sergeant friend who was talking into a two-way radio.

But what really caught her eye was the sight of Sam seated on the settee next to a shrinking, fair-haired girl of about sixteen and as pretty as a flower. He was holding her hand and gazing down at her raptly.

'Ah, Jane,' Liam said noticing her, 'come in. This is Elizabeth Green who lives down the road and had the misfortune to encounter the two louts who chased you. Luckily for her, Sam was coming home at the same time.'

Elizabeth Green had raised scared blue eyes to Jane but at the mention of Sam she turned to him with every evidence of hero-worship in them. Sam smiled reassuringly down at her and looked very much as if he'd like to take her in his arms and hold her very close.

Jane blinked then smiled to herself, a faint wry smile as she thought, So much for older women.

Half an hour later, she was alone with Liam, however, as all concerned including Sam relocated themselves to Elizabeth's home.

Liam was the first to speak. 'This place is becoming like a railway station but at least that's one problem sorted out. I told you it wouldn't last.'

'Ah, fickle heart,' Jane said. 'Is it a Benedict trait to be so smitten on first encounters?'

He smiled slightly. 'It would appear so.'

'But what are the odds on these things lasting?' she said lightly. 'Last night he was smitten with me.'

'He probably always realised you were a bit out of his league but wouldn't admit it. Like a drink?'

'Yes, please,' she said wearily and pulled the pins out her hair then kicked off her shoes and sank on to the settee. 'Poor kid,' she murmured and added, 'It's about time they caught them, isn't it?'

'I reckon they will this time. Sam got the number of the car they drove off in.'

Jane laid her head back and chuckled with some satisfaction. 'They must have got a shock when he turned up. Just a pity it couldn't have been you.'

'Why?' he said idly and handed her a drink.

'Because you're more impressive even than Sam. You have the weight of maturity, and, just sometimes, something very cold and determined about you which Sam lacks as yet.'

He sat down opposite and didn't reply although their eyes locked suddenly as Jane sat up abruptly. 'I... oh, hell,' she said very quietly and put a hand to her mouth. 'If you must know, if you really want honesty, Liam Benedict, I might not scare you but you scare me.'

'Why?'

'Because I've got this feeling I'm being railroaded into things,' she said helplessly.

'I told you I wouldn't force you into anything.' He stared down at his drink then looked at her wryly, 'Other than the odd kiss. I apologise for that one.'

'Ah, but I'm beginning to perceive that brute force isn't your only weapon——'

'It's not a weapon of mine at all other than in a fair fight, Jane,' he said evenly. 'And, apart from Elizabeth Green, I can't at this moment call to mind anyone I know who would be more unevenly matched to me than you.'

'Apologies to the bench, I'll rephrase.' But she sighed suddenly and instead of rephrasing said, 'Don't you understand what I mean at all?'

'You're free and over twenty-one, Jane,' he pointed out.

'Say—just say I decided to experiment a little...' She broke off and blinked at the glass in her hand and broke into a sudden cold sweat, unable for the life of her to imagine what had prompted her. 'Forget it,' she muttered, and went to get up.

He stirred and glanced at his watch. 'If you'd like to—why not?'

'Oh, I was only theorising,' she said hastily.

'Nor was I about to leap on you,' he returned gravely.

She did stand up in her stockinged feet. 'What, then?' she enquired tartly.

'I'm going to a ball tonight. The invitation included a partner. You could be it.'

'A ball? Where? Why?' She bit her lip.

'At the Sheraton, in aid of charity, and I've been asked to deputise for the guest speaker who was taken ill this morning.'

Jane stared at him.

'You told me yourself I sound quite well-educated; I'll try not to let the side down.' A malicious little glint of humour lit his eyes.

'I didn't...I did apologise for that,' Jane said stiffly.

'So you did,' he murmured.

'And *you* gave me to understand I needn't have,' she swept on, suddenly irrationally irritated. 'But anyway, I'm not a very good dancer.'

'We don't have to dance. I'm not too sure how my knee will hold up to dancing, anyway. Do you own a ballgown?'

'I ... yes, I do, but I've never worn it,' she admitted ungraciously. 'I still don't see the point of going to a ball if you don't dance——'

'Then I'll show you. You have just under an hour to get ready, *if* you're so minded, Miss Mathieson.' His teeth gleamed in a faint smile. 'But if you're going to look like Daniel going to the lion's den or the way you looked before you stepped on to a boat—although that changed, didn't it?' he said meditatively. 'But if you're going to make me feel I twisted your arm in any way, let's——'

'Make you feel as if you've twisted my arm!' she marvelled. 'Just tell me how to do that, Mr Benedict?' She stared at him broodingly.

'Jane, come of your own free will or don't come at all,' he said with infuriating patience. 'But time's running out. You were the one, after all, who expressed a desire to experiment, but perhaps you meant you'd rather do it in private?' He raised an eyebrow at her. 'Once I've made the speech, I could leave and come back here fairly early.'

'I'll come,' Jane said with a considerable degree of fatalism.

CHAPTER SIX

THE dress was black and strapless with a long waist and yards of chiffon in the skirt. There was a creamy silk camellia between her breasts and a matching one pinned to her loose hair. Jane stared at herself in the mirror then twitched her gaze away impatiently and picked up her velvet coat.

Liam was ready and waiting, looking incredibly tall and distinguished in a dark dinner suit. 'Very nice,' she said involuntarily.

'Thank you,' he replied wryly. 'You look exquisite, on the other hand. You should wear that dress more often.'

She grimaced. 'To be honest, I bought it in a moment of aberration about two years ago. But since doing the deed I never felt it was quite me, apart from the lack of ball invitations in the interim—what about Sam?'

His gaze rested on her pale, smooth shoulders and there was something faintly ironic in it. But he said, 'Sam rang while you were in the shower. He's been invited to have dinner with the Greens.'

Jane grinned. 'Then let's go.'

'And so, ladies and gentlemen, I commend this worthy cause to you.'

There was a storm of applause, for Liam's speech had been humorous, he'd held the large audience in the palm of his hand, and, above all, it hadn't been too long. A very accomplished performance, Jane thought, as he

wove his way back to their table, being stopped fre-
quently on the way. I shall certainly guard against making
snap judgements in future...

'Like to dance?'

She turned with a little jolt. It was Liam. 'I thought...'
She stopped as the lights were dimmed and the band
struck up.

'We mooted several possibilities—did we make any
cast-iron decisions?' He pulled his chair out and sat down
but turned towards her and raised his champagne glass
to her before drinking from it. His eyes never left her
face.

'But I told you I wasn't a very good dancer,' she said
in a suddenly flustered undertone.

He shrugged. 'No one will notice. For that matter my
knee doesn't allow me to leap about.'

'I...when will they know it's all right? You don't limp
or anything.'

'If it doesn't give out on me, they'll know,' he murmured, but there was just enough light to see the teasing
glint in his blue eyes.

'That doesn't sound very satisfactory to me. And,'
Jane said slowly, 'you did *say* we needn't dance.'

'I was wrong.' He stood up and held out his hand.

She put hers into it uncertainly.

Half an hour later, she looked up suddenly into his eyes
and said huskily, 'You must be a very good partner—
usually I'm all tense and it's as if every drop of what
rhythm I do possess has drained away.'

That little glint of irony she'd seen before glinted in
his eyes but he said, 'We could try something a bit different now, if you'd like.' And right on cue the band
changed tempo.

'Oh, but your knee,' she protested.

'I'll tell you when it's had enough,' he promised. 'Ready?'

Jane sang softly at two o'clock in the morning and pirouetted across their lounge. She came to a sudden standstill right in front of Liam and had to smile up at him. 'I also had more champagne than I'm accustomed to,' she confessed. 'I don't know how to thank you for making a ball—occasions which haven't until now been that enjoyable—so memorable, but thanks anyway and I'd better get to bed otherwise I'll be a wreck in the morning.'

But she didn't move because the last thing she wanted to do was leave him, she discovered. It was as if not only the music and the dancing but also the feel of being in his arms, the way her breasts had felt when she'd brushed against him, the way his hands had felt on her waist had all been leading up to something more—and she knew suddenly exactly what it was. She wanted to be kissed, she really wanted his hands on her body again, his strength surrounding her and causing her to feel soft and helpless and kissable.

And as it all struck her, her eyes dilated, her lips parted, and she tore her gaze away agitatedly.

His eyes narrowed. 'What's wrong?'

'Nothing,' she said raggedly. 'Nothing. Goodnight.'

But he caught her wrist as she went to turn away. 'No. Tell me.'

'Liam,' she licked her lips and took a breath, 'I...' She tried to break his grip but it was impossible and she got into a worse state as his gaze dropped to her breasts which were rising and falling agitatedly.

'Jane,' he released her wrist abruptly and his eyes came back to rest on her face, 'there's something I don't understand about you. At times, it wouldn't be hard to believe you're a virgin.' He stared searchingly into her eyes.

She blushed brilliantly and correspondingly, said rather fiercely, 'So? What if I am?'

His teeth shut hard and a nerve flickered in his jaw before he shook his head and said, 'Why the *hell* didn't you want me to know?'

Her shoulders slumped suddenly. 'Twenty-four-year-old virgins can be laughed at or held up to ridicule,' she said a little hollowly, and put a hand to her cheek which was still hot. 'And this one,' she added barely audibly, as the irony of the situation struck her forcibly, 'is, well— I think I ought to just go to bed. Again.' She grimaced.

'I'm not laughing,' he said quietly, 'but—this puts a different light on things.'

'Don't you kiss virgins?' she whispered.

His lips twisted. 'Very seldom.'

'Even when they want it...?' She bit her lip, then began to feel annoyed, and on a sudden impulse she put her hands up and clutched his lapels, stood on tiptoe and kissed him, a mere peck on the lips, but before she could retreat he grasped her hands, murmured something inaudible, and pulled her into his arms, but he didn't kiss her. Instead, he trailed his fingers lightly up her bare arm, cupped her shoulder then stroked her throat and behind her ear.

She trembled but didn't want him to stop so she closed her eyes and he didn't for a moment more, then she thought he sighed and his hand fell away as he said with that odd, twisted little smile, 'What are you thinking, Jane?'

Her lashes lifted and her eyes were a little dazed. 'I'm not, I'm *feeling*,' she murmured. 'So far it's rather nice. If,' the corners of her mouth dimpled suddenly, 'I had to write the definitive essay on it, for example, I would comment favourably. Is it nice for you?'

His fingers slid into her hair, 'Nicer than you have the slightest idea of, my dear, but...let's leave it at that.' And he bent his head and kissed her as briefly as she'd kissed him, and released her.

Her lips parted. 'Why?' she whispered.

'There's such a thing as taking unfair advantage, Jane, that's all. Go to bed. I'm sure that in the morning you'll be glad you did.'

'I don't understand.'

'That's the problem. Sleep well.' He stared down at her for a moment then turned abruptly away.

'Sleep well,' she repeated as she closed her bedroom door and added slowly and carefully to her bemused reflection in the mirror, '*That* might be a problem.'

She shivered and wrapped her arms around herself and went on staring into the mirror. There were tired shadows now visibly stamped beneath her eyes and her mouth was naked of any lipstick. And there was the humiliation of a pretty brutal rebuff considering the events that had led up to tonight, in her heart. Why? she wondered bleakly. I could hardly have capitulated more completely—it must have to do with being a virgin. Perhaps he finds them dull and boring? But I'm still exactly the same person he purported to be very attracted to. She closed her eyes and reflected that she should probably be feeling very angry but instead she felt drained and sad, and it was all quite new and foreign to her...

* * *

Breakfast was again an awkward affair although helped by Sam who appeared oblivious to the tension in the air and was apparently not at all surprised to see his cousin formally dressed in a grey suit and waistcoat, white shirt and navy-blue tie.

In fact he was discussing it with Liam as Jane emerged. 'You don't mind me staying on even if you're going back to work, do you, Liam?' he was in the middle of saying.

'No. I gather Elizabeth Green is also on vacation. School vacation,'' Liam added somewhat pointedly.

'She's in her last year,' Sam confided. 'I asked her parents' permission to take her to the movies this afternoon. They thought it would be a good idea—take her mind off what happened yesterday.'

Jane sat down at the table and thought privately that it would not be long before Elizabeth Green had little else on her mind but Sam Benedict if that was not already the case. Then it occurred to her that she was being superior with little cause considering how Liam Benedict was occupying her mind. She shot him a veiled glance, but it was like viewing a brick wall, she realised with an odd little jolt. Because, she also realised, even when it had been a furious rapport on her part or a sardonic one on his, it had always been there virtually from the time they'd first laid eyes on each other. But now there was only a polite indifference that was almost tangible— who the hell does he think he is? she marvelled, her curious sense of desolation turning to one of extreme ire.

They left the house together by an awkward mischance. 'I gather,' Jane said, tossing her head and unable to control her feelings, 'I offended you somehow or other last night. If you'd like to tell me in words of one syllable what I did wrong——'

'You did nothing wrong, Jane,' he said drily. 'Watch your step.'

'Oh...' She ground her teeth, reached the bottom step safely and swung round to face him. 'So it's all off? I must say that's a relief to me, Liam!'

'Is it?' He regarded her dispassionately. 'Good. I'd hate to think of you going to work all bitter and twisted.'

She made a furious, disgusted sound and flung away from him towards the garage. She also drove to work at a reckless speed.

They didn't see a lot of each other over the next week, which was just as well, Jane reflected, as her delayed anger stayed with her. But, inevitably perhaps, it cooled finally and then turned to a rather miserable kind of confusion. A few days of that, however, left her feeling limp and oddly restless, and, from being angry with him, she realised again how acutely aware of him she was. She only had to look at his hands, for example, to remember the feel of his fingers on her skin, and he only had to cross the room to remind her how light he was on his feet for a big man. And when his gaze did rest on her briefly she found herself wondering if he still thought she was attractive or whether her tantrums and taunts had overlaid a shrewish stamp on her and that was all he saw now. She came home one afternoon and discovered Sam kissing Elizabeth Green on the settee, very gently, and couldn't miss the rapture in her blue eyes even while they hurriedly drew apart, and discovered herself filled with a kind of lonely melancholy that made her long to go to Liam and say, 'You started this, you created this lonely void...' She discovered she felt cold a lot, colder than she usually felt in winter. Nor did the events of the next day help in the slightest.

One of the senior partners, Peter Simpson, invited her to lunch, to congratulate her, he said, on the fine job she was doing. This both surprised and dismayed her. Surprised her because she hadn't felt she'd been doing a particularly fine job lately at all, and dismayed her because another casualty of her state of mind seemed to be her social skills—she could think of nothing worse in fact than having to be an intelligent yet amusing companion to a man she didn't know that well but knew that was what he would expect. One didn't get asked to lunch to be a bore, she was sure.

Laura, however, was thrilled.

'Darling, this is an *honour*,' she said bracingly. 'Why are you looking so glum?'

'I—I don't know.'

'Really, Jane, you amaze me sometimes. I would have thought you were intensely ambitious, I really would have, but lately I can't help wondering. Now look here, buck up—at least you look the part. That suit is divine on you, believe me, so why don't you go and have a wash and a brush up, spray on a bit of perfume? After all, when you have all the guns, it's criminal not to use them!'

Jane stared at her. 'If you imagine for *one* moment that I have any intention of——'

'I don't, not you,' Laura responded wryly, 'but look at it this way; it has to help to look your best.'

Unfortunately this rang an echoing chord in Jane's mind but she took herself off to the powder-room nevertheless more in an effort to wring some enthusiasm into herself than for any other reason. But, once there, she stared at her image in the mirror for a long time. The suit Laura thought divine was a slim, simple but elegant Perri Cutten pure wool crêpe creation in a soft apricot and she'd actually bought it for James and Amanda's wedding then decided that although it was a bit more colourful than what she normally wore to work it had cost an arm and a leg and therefore should earn its keep. And she had put it on that morning, she reminded herself, to try to lift her mood. But not even the lovely apricot could disguise the fact that there were faint shadows beneath her eyes and an expression in them that was disturbing. She sighed, then squared her shoulders, took out her make-up and set to work.

And it was, as Laura had predicted, a help to walk into the very expensive restaurant her companion had chosen, knowing that she was impeccably groomed, even head-turningly so. It was no help at all though that they should walk in, on the heels virtually, of Liam and a similarly elegant and well-groomed woman of about thirty.

What was even more disturbing was that her senior partner almost fell on Liam with delighted cries of recognition and phrases such as, 'Wonderful to see you back in circulation, old son...are you all over it?' and so on. But the *coup de grâce* came when he turned to introduce Jane and she looked for the first time straight into Liam's eyes and murmured that they knew each other...

'Rather well as a matter of fact, Peter,' he said for her as she ran out of words and could only run her tongue over her delicately apricot-shaded lips nervously. 'Jane's sister is married to my brother——'

'Then let's join up for lunch,' Peter Simpson said delightedly, and added provocatively and with little subtlety, 'You haven't introduced us to your companion, Liam.'

Liam smiled a touch drily. 'This is Sandra Gillespie, Sandra—Peter Simpson and Jane Mathieson. Sandra is a colleague,' he added.

She may be, Jane thought drearily several times during the lunch, but she's also an intelligent, amusing companion, she's extremely attractive, and she covered up her initial lack of enthusiasm at having to share Liam Benedict very well. Whereas I'm finding it hard to string two words together, I'm all worked up just to be sitting opposite him and having to watch him also being intelligent and amusing in his own laid-back kind of way, having to see the way he looks at me occasionally as if he knows exactly what I'm going through and is doing his best to cover for me... And on top of it all I'm in the ridiculous position of hating the way this woman, a woman I've never laid eyes on before, can do what I can't do with such a light touch. Can let her interest in Liam show, and she is, but without sacrificing her social skills, her sleep, her—heavens knows what. Perhaps I should take a leaf out of her book, or I should have... It's too late now.

It was as they were leaving after an ordeal that had left Jane feeling exhausted that she found herself standing on the pavement alone with Liam as the other two stopped to chat to the proprietor. And found that it hurt more than she would have believed that they should be standing there like two virtual strangers.

She swallowed, glanced behind her then turned to him with a crooked little smile that cost her enormous effort. 'Life's full of coincidences, isn't it? You didn't tell me you knew Peter.'

He studied her thoughtfully. 'Life is,' he agreed finally. 'I'm sorry——' he gestured ' —about this.'

'Oh, it wasn't your fault,' Jane said brightly, but it came out sounding brittle. 'Have you known Sandra long?'

'She came to work for us not long before the accident.'

'She seems to be delighted to have you back...' Oh, God, I didn't say that, did I? she thought with a tinge of panic. I must be going round the bend... 'I mean,' she amended jerkily, 'she seems very nice.'

'She is. She's also very efficient. Jane——' He stopped and sighed briefly. 'Here they come.'

And to her relief they did and within a few minutes her ordeal was over. But despite what she felt was a poor performance at lunch, she seemed to have gone up another notch in Peter Simpson's estimation because of her association with Liam Benedict—which struck her as being incredibly ironic.

She also stayed back at the office and worked very late in a conscious bid to avoid seeing Liam that night— which was successful—and made the decision to move out as soon as possible.

It was the next morning that she picked up the phone on her desk to hear Laura say there was a gentleman who wanted to see her but wouldn't give his name.

'Send him in,' Jane said listlessly.

'But——'

'Laura, I doubt if he's here to knock me off; he probably just wants the complete privacy of not having his name bandied about an office full of gossiping secretaries.'

'Why, Jane—that's better! I thought you'd lost all your spirit lately but I see it's not so. I'll be on call, however,' Laura added cryptically.

'Thank you,' Jane had the grace to say. She put the phone down with a shrug, reached for her jacket hanging on the back of her chair and slipped into it. She rose as the door opened and extended her hand as a tall, middle-aged man casually dressed in khaki trousers, desert boots and a check shirt, a man with a good-looking, tanned face and green eyes, entered, but the way he stopped for a moment and the way his eyes narrowed before he closed the door with an effort, as if he had to drag his gaze away, caused a *frisson* to touch her nerves, and for a moment she wondered if he did have some devious intent.

Then he said, 'Jane? I don't suppose you recognise me but I'm...your father. I've lived overseas ever since your mother and I separated and I'm afraid this is only a flying visit but if you don't hate me it could be the first of more...'

She didn't get home until after ten o'clock that night and it wasn't easy to negotiate the back steps. Liam was home but there was no sign of Sam. She barely glanced at Liam, however, as she made her way with an effort to her bedroom. She closed her door and leant against it for a moment then, without bothering to turn on the light, sank into the armchair.

That was how Liam found her, still huddled there some moments later, when he opened the door and flicked on the light. She blinked then laid her head back with a sigh. 'What do you want? By the way, I've decided to move out of here as soon as I can find a place.'

He stared at the tear marks on her cheeks and answered her question with a question, 'What's happened? You look...drunk.'

'Do I?' She laughed hollowly. 'Perhaps that's what I should have done. Got drunk.'

'Why?'

But she dropped her head into her hands suddenly. 'Go away, please, Liam.'

He didn't. He squatted down beside the chair instead and prised her hands away. 'Tell me, Jane.'

'Why should I?' she retorted. 'There's no reason for me to tell you anything—we're——'

'All the same, you're going to.' He held her wrists in her lap and studied her steadily. 'Start talking, Jane.'

She licked a tear off her lip and shrugged but more came, a torrent. 'My father paid me a flying visit, if you must know,' she wept finally. 'Do you know why I didn't know if he was dead or alive? Our own mother intercepted every last letter and birthday card he ever sent us. And he let her, he didn't once come and *force* her to let us see him.' She laughed a little wildly, 'What's more, he's got three kids by his second wife.'

Some time later, Liam stirred and stared down at her, cradled in his arms and he smoothed some damp hair off her face. 'Feeling better?'

'Yes.'

'Then I'm going to make you something to eat and you can tell me the rest of it.'

'I don't know what else there is to tell,' she said as she ate the sandwiches he'd made and sipped a cup of tea.

'Did you let him know how bitter *you* felt, for example?'

'No, I don't think so. It didn't really hit me until he'd gone, anyway. We only had a couple of hours together and he did most of the talking.'

'Did he tell you why—it happened the way it did?'

She was silent for a long time. 'Yes, he did. He told me how he discovered they were basically unsuited pretty early on in the marriage. He said my mother was lovely and sexy but they had nothing else in common and she made him feel incredibly caged in—whereas he needed a lot of space and solitude, she needed to be needed all the time. My mother was,' she spread her hands, 'not an intellectual, which he obviously is, but she was also...proud of it,' she said painfully. 'That's the difference between her and Amanda. Amanda isn't proud and prickly and determinedly an *"I am what I am"* kind of person. I think my mother always was. Anyway,' she went on, 'the crisis came when my grandfather, my father's father, died and left him quite a lot of money. That's when his ambition to see the world suddenly became a reality—he was also a lawyer but he'd always had a hankering to do something for the less fortunate, so he applied for and got a job with a worldwide charity that meant living in different, often third world countries and so on. But my mother nearly had a heart attack and refused point-blank. He said,' her voice trembled, 'that that was when he had to go. Because he...her small-town mentality on top of their other differences was bringing *his* worst aspects out. He said he was horrified to discover he could barely stop himself from...from...' She couldn't go on.

'Stop himself from dealing violently with her,' Liam said.

'Yes,' Jane whispered.

'Then he probably did the right thing.'

'Yes,' she agreed. 'He did a lot of right things, in fact. I didn't know this, but he supported us even after the divorce. Of course he would have to, by law, but I'd somehow assumed that he'd taken off into the wide blue yonder and left her to do it all.' She lifted her eyes to his. 'I'm extremely naïve, sometimes. I never queried the impression she gave us to the contrary; she *hated* to talk about it and when she died there was nothing among her papers... If *only*——' her voice broke '—he'd substituted some...'

'Drink your tea. Jane,' he flexed his shoulders, 'if you've done a stint in the family court, you must know what a commonplace story this is.'

'Oh, I do——'

'And know,' he continued, 'that your mother, in her bitterness, would have hated him to have any contact with you, especially after he remarried and she didn't. She might have even put up all sorts of obstacles. Had you never come across the futility of having to give court orders to protect visiting rights, of the harm it does to children if the police have to step in, in those situations?'

'Yes, I thought I'd seen it all, Liam,' she responded wearily. 'It still doesn't help me to believe that he couldn't have come up with some way of...' She shrugged again. 'I asked him about that, actually. He said more or less what you've just said and that he'd never lost his fear of those violent impulses my mother had aroused in him and that he'd concluded that while the situation was not *right* it might be the safest way for us all.'

'Do you remember any of it, Jane?' Liam queried with a faint frown in his eyes.

'I remember the rows, I remember wanting to tell them to stop it because I loved them both, I remember... I've never forgotten how safe I used to feel when he hugged me and I remember how we used to talk about all sorts of things even though I was so young, and how it used to annoy my mother—funnily enough I don't remember the final parting. I mean,' she stared at her cup unseeingly, 'there just was this realisation that he wasn't coming back. I don't think I made a scene, I just knew.'

'Have you——' he paused and fiddled with his own cup then raised his head '—had time to work out how it all helped to shape the person you are, Jane?'

'Oh, yes,' she said bleakly. 'I've had hours. I took the afternoon off and went to a movie and I went to another one this evening. I don't remember what either of them were.'

'Tell me.'

She stood up and took her cup and plate over to the sink and with her back to him, said slowly, 'I suppose you have to have some convictions on that old question of heredity over environment but I can't help wondering if I didn't inherit what he called his need for space and solitude that my mother tried so desperately to trample, apparently. Perhaps that accounts for my... failure to want to leap into bed with anyone yet. I can see now that I must have subconsciously recognised how his intellectualism was an affront to her because she couldn't match it and I think all my burning zeal and ambition has its roots in wanting to prove I could match his mind. Now,' she turned at last, 'I can't help thinking it was a waste of time from that point of view.'

'Why?'

She pushed her hair back dispiritedly. 'Well—he was honest and more than ready to take the lion's share of the blame; I think it *has* all haunted him and caused him a lot of agony but I've just got this feeling it's too late to be much help to me, knowing it all, I mean.'

'That could change. It's been a big shock, Jane. In time, you'll probably find yourself accepting and understanding.'

She thought for a moment then she said with a queer little gesture, 'So time is what it takes. Do you think it will also work for me in regard to you, Liam?'

Their eyes locked across the room. 'What do you mean?'

'I mean,' she crossed her arms and leant back against the sink, 'you obviously don't think I merit an explanation for what happened between us. You're convinced I can't understand, now anyway—at least, that's what you said.'

There was another long silence, and, although she held his gaze calmly, a pulse started to beat at the base of her throat in a nervous little tattoo.

'That's true.' He let his gaze drift over her beautiful tweed suit and elegant brown shoes, and her naked, pale and still tear-stained face, her loose hair, which she raked back with a sudden impatient gesture, then he went on evenly, 'I didn't think you'd understand then, but you might now, although——'

'Try me.'

He moved his shoulders restlessly. 'You've had a traumatic day, Jane——'

'I've had a traumatic week, Liam. Look, I'll admit freely that against my will, against my better judgement, you—got me in. I'm not blaming you for it either, as you yourself pointed out I'm free and over twenty-one, but I can't help being mystified and it really would be kinder to tell me whether, once I looked like caving in, the challenge went out of it for you, for example, or whether I was so useless about it all that you felt like a kindergarten teacher—I can agree that would be quite enough to turn most men off but why do you assume I can't understand any of that?'

'I'm not assuming anything like that—in fact it was none of those things——'

'Then *tell* me!' Her eyes were a dark, intense green and a nerve flickered in her jaw.

He hesitated. 'Sit down.'

'*No*. Believe me, I can take it like a man, Liam—don't patronise me any more than you already have!'

'I wonder,' he said barely audibly, and sprawled back in his chair with a sigh. 'As a matter of fact, it's all really only fallen into place for me. I think the reason you stayed a virgin so long is because all your life you've been looking for a father figure.' He stopped as she went paler and swayed slightly but she grabbed the sink and steadied herself.

He waited then went on. 'But while virginity can be a conscious choice or a subconscious one or an imposed one, it's also going against nature and I think it was starting to make you feel uneasy. Helped along perhaps by having your *younger* sister steal a friend you saw as an intellectual equal and steal him moreover with the kind of arts you despised. I just happened along,' he said drily, 'at a crucial time.'

She did sit down this time. And said huskily, 'Are you trying to say in a roundabout, polite sort of way that my hormones have finally fought their way to the top, Liam?'

He smiled but without amusement.

'Where does this leave you, though?' she queried eventually when he made no further comment. 'Regarding *me*,' she added so that there should be no misunderstanding, no beating around the bush. 'Or has Sandra Gillespie relieved you of the problem?'

He drummed his fingers on the table a couple of times then said coolly, 'Why were you lunching with Peter Simpson yesterday, Jane?'

She opened her mouth, closed it then said stiffly, 'It was purely business.'

'Then you should have no difficulty in believing Sandra and I were doing the same.'

Jane bit her lip and thought of saying, 'It might have been for *you* but it wasn't purely business for her,' but just thinking it made her feel bitchy and jealous so she said instead, 'Well, where does it leave you, then? In regard to me.'

He thought for a moment then said wryly, 'In a slightly unenviable position, Jane. But I'll cope. When are you moving out?'

She gasped. 'But...'

'You did mention it earlier,' he reminded her with a trace of irony. 'Not that I expect you to rush it after this shock, but...' He shrugged.

'But I don't understand——' She stopped. 'I mean, I thought it was all over for you but you just said...' She looked at him helplessly.

'Well, I think it needs to be, don't you?' he said with a sudden glint of humour. 'For several reasons. Look, I can understand how devastated you feel at the moment and that's one reason why I didn't want to go into this now.' He pushed his chair back impatiently and stood up, the glint of humour disappearing. 'But I'm not the right person to help you through it, perhaps only your father is if he's staying around long enough, or, if not, go with him—forget your career, it'll keep. This could be more important to you than anything else. The other thing is, I may not be a rapist in disguise as you once thought, nor do I sleep with any woman simply because she's available, but I'm not a celibate saint, either, Jane,' he said deliberately.

Her first reaction was an inward shiver of hurt to this stark statement. But then she tossed her head and tilted her chin at him. 'You're also a bit of a quitter, aren't you, Liam?'

It wasn't often Liam Benedict allowed himself to be moved to anger, she knew, but for a moment a rough, tough version of it blazed in his eyes and his mouth set in a hard line.

This time she shivered visibly, but, being Jane and born with a certain set of genes that might have come more from her mother than her father, she went on stubbornly and with her own brand of belligerence, 'I think a lot of what you said about me is probably true. I have always felt bereft without my father and his approval, I think both of us did, but whereas Amanda reached out to people for affection I went the other way—but that's not what I want from you.'

'What do you *want*?' he said softly.

A flood of colour burnt her cheeks but she persisted doggedly. 'And I think it's ridiculously simplistic to blame my hormones—in fact I much prefer your original theory,' she said with considerable irony. 'The one about needing the right man,' she added gently. 'Do you remember saying that to me? But perhaps the whole problem *is* much simpler. Wasn't I enough of a challenge to you after all, Liam?'

CHAPTER SEVEN

THE silence lasted two whole minutes as Liam Benedict gave no indication of his feelings while he studied Jane with a thoroughness that resembled being put under a high-powered microscope. But she bore this impassive scrutiny bravely.

Then he said drily, 'By the way, Sam's been recalled. His mother decided a bit of space between him and Elizabeth might be a good idea.'

'Oh,' Jane said in a disconcerted kind of way. 'I'll miss him and I don't think he'd do anything wrong, would he? But what's that got to do with me and all this?' She blinked at him.

He said deliberately. 'You're lonely, Jane. I think Sam and I provided a kind of family for you but you shouldn't try to build it into more or what it's not.'

Jane stared at him for a long moment then she rested her arms on the table and laid her head on them wearily. 'All right, I'm lonely,' she murmured. 'If you must know,' she looked up briefly and her eyes were wet and bitter, 'I don't think I've ever felt lonelier than I do right now but,' she sat up, 'don't worry. I know when I'm beaten. For the record, though, there's just one last thing I'd like to add—you say you still feel . . . I presume you meant you still feel attracted to me—I don't believe that. Or, at least, I don't think it could have been a very strong attraction, perhaps it's even become more pity than anything else. I just wish,' she brushed her eyes impatiently, 'you'd been honest, that's all. I think I'll go to bed——'

'Jane...' He said her name harshly and she shivered because his face had set into those rough, tough lines again and he turned away and said suddenly with his back to her, 'If you really want honesty, I'll give it to you.' He swung round. 'There's something you obviously don't know about me, something that in the normal course of events might not have mattered, but, as things are, something that's really ironic. I have a lot in common with your father, you see. The only difference is that I have a son instead of two daughters.'

'You're...you're married!' Jane gasped, her eyes wide and stunned. 'But——'

'I'm divorced and have been for years. My ex-wife and son live in New Zealand.'

She stared at him wordlessly.

'I too married a girl who, well, let's just say it was a mistake, it included an unplanned pregnancy and two years of living hell for both of us,' he said drily.

Still Jane couldn't speak.

He shrugged. 'So. We can all make mistakes—we're both older and wiser now and Rory is ten and although I haven't abandoned him I can understand exactly how your father felt—I also know what it's like to be afraid of living in a relationship with a woman who has nothing in common with you or vice versa, let's be fair, and, because of Rory, I know how *you* feel. I also have to be honest and tell you that while intellectually one can tell oneself there has to be the right woman somewhere, the one who can make it work, it's not easy to make yourself *believe* it. In other words, Jane, I'm very cynical about marriage now, and the constraints and the awful pressures of it, and particularly cynical about my capacity for it. I also have to apologise to you because when I started this I...' He paused and sighed suddenly.

'Go on,' she whispered.

'I—it was as if I was at a crossroads in my life,' he said rather bleakly, 'and everything seemed pretty flat and boring, probably because I'd been pretty bored and,' he shrugged, 'out of sorts for a while. And my first impressions of you *were* that you were the kind of tough, independent, experienced woman who didn't like to go down without a fight—which suited—well, my frame of mind. That was *also* what you more or less told me.'

Jane closed her eyes. 'Then you found out...'

He smiled but unamusedly. 'I'd already started to wonder. I couldn't believe how unaware you were and of course it's the only thing that makes sense of you— I just wish to God I'd stopped earlier and taken note of those question marks, and the implications,' he said levelly.

'What implications?' she said with an effort.

'That there had to be deeply entrenched reasons for the way you were that would make it impossible for you to play the game the way I wanted it.' He paused then said deliberately, 'You must have seen it time and time again, Jane. No—ties.'

'Oh. Yes,' Jane said then frowned. 'I probably wouldn't make a good mistress, I mean I don't really believe in that kind of thing, well, I don't think I do,' she said perplexedly, 'but aren't we discounting the possibility——?' She stopped abruptly and her eyes widened. 'You're really afraid I'm falling in love with you, aren't you, Liam?' she whispered.

'On my past record I'm a lousy bet to fall in love with but especially for someone like you with your past record of being deserted——'

'Just now you tried to tell me I *wasn't* falling in love. That all I was suffering from was rejection and lone-liness, and a sense of unease with my anachronistic estate,' she countered. 'You can't have it both ways, Liam.'

'Jane—whether you did fall in love or only convinced yourself you had because of all that, *whatever*, I'm still probably the worst person for you.'

'Well, you've warned me, haven't you? So I'll know better than to expect you to want to rush me to the altar, always assuming I want to be so rushed. To be perfectly honest, I doubt very much that I would make good mar-riage material, either—I might be better mistress ma-terial after all. Don't tell me you haven't noticed that I'm short-tempered, opinionated, not to mention a cynic in my own right, but never let it be said,' she said with considerable irony, 'that I'd forced you into anything, Liam.'

His eyes narrowed. 'What did you have in mind, Jane?'

She stared at him. 'I had in mind us taking up where we left off, that's all. I...well,' she said with a strangely twisted little smile, 'I hadn't got down to analysing all the whys and the wherefores not to mention the *impli-cations* but, unfortunately, Liam, you backed off too late and embarrassing as it is for me to have to admit this, I'm now possessed of a curiosity that's making my life very difficult. I can't get you out of my mind, I can't sleep, I feel cold all the time—I can't imagine why. Is it a symptom of frustration, do you think? You should know—it was your expertise that achieved it. And all this,' she gestured, taking in the night and all they'd been discussing, 'hasn't changed that.'

He swore beneath his breath.

'Did she love you?' Jane said abruptly. 'Did *she* want you to stay—your wife?'

His mouth hardened. 'She—yes. At the time, but mainly because she was looking down the barrel of being a single parent. She's since remarried and is much happier than she ever was with me.'

Jane grimaced. 'Perhaps you might even achieve that for me. Hand me a suitable husband; who knows? You seem to be good at that.' She flashed him a green glance filled with sudden contempt.

The result of her words was surprising. He relaxed visibly and his eyes were suddenly amused. 'Are you sure you don't prefer fighting me than anything else, Jane? I think we'd make much better sparring partners than lovers.'

A blaze of anger so intense that it took her by surprise swept through Jane and she stood up precipitately and hissed through her teeth, 'Yes, I want to fight you, damn you, Liam Benedict! Who the hell do you think you are? I'm not just some object to be toyed with when you feel bored and flat, even if you *were* convalescing, and then dropped on the next whim—how could you do that to any woman when you know there's going to be no future in it? How low is that? You've made me virtually *grovel* and all you can do is laugh at me—I must have been mad! And I won't be leaving tomorrow or the next day— I'll be doing it right now——'

'Jane——'

'Don't...don't say a word,' she stammered. 'I despise you and thank heavens I realised it before...before... I could hit you, I really could! But I'll do this instead.' And so saying she picked up her cup and flung it at him.

He dodged it with ease and took a step towards her but she reached for the saucer and threw that as well and had her hand on the sugar bowl but in one long stride he was beside her and he forced the bowl out of her fingers and pulled her into his arms. 'Stop it,' he commanded.

'*No*. I——'

'Then I will. If you really want to experiment, Jane, here's your chance, but don't say I didn't warn you.' His mouth closed on hers.

Shock held her stunned and rigid and her lips parted in a soundless gasp, and from that moment she was being kissed with a merciless, mocking kind of expertise that took her breath away and took ruthless advantage of his strength as opposed to her sudden helplessness. Then it was over as abruptly as it had begun. He lifted his head, studied her white, frightened face and bruised mouth and he said something beneath his breath and picked her up as she slumped in his arms.

He carried her to the settee and set her down much as he'd used to once, with her legs up, and then sat down beside her.

'That was unforgivable,' he said with an effort. 'I'm sorry, Jane.'

She licked her lips and looked up into the dark blue of his eyes. 'You're right,' she said huskily. 'It wasn't a very nice thing to do. I'm just wondering how much I asked for it, though. I mean, I don't suppose you could have thrown things back at me. I've made an awful mess of this, haven't I?' She frowned. 'I think I ought to go to bed and try to put this day behind me. Sorry. But could you just tell me one thing?'

He observed her narrowly. 'You don't think your mind has gone into overdrive, Jane? Because of this awful day and——'

'I do, but I *definitely* won't be able to sleep with this question going round and round in my mind—was that why you did it?' She gazed at him, and, perceiving no reaction, tried to explain. 'I mean, did you kiss me because it was the only way to shut me up, sort of, without slapping me or throwing things back—the only way a man can retaliate in other words—or did you really want to?'

'I...' His lips twitched involuntarily. 'It was a mixture of both.'

Jane laid her head back and sighed. 'I didn't react properly, did I?'

'Didn't you?' He raised a quizzical eyebrow.

'If you can believe what you read,' she said gloomily, 'I should have been overcome by your masterful, manly presence and melted into your arms—I should have been quite disarmed!'

'Where did you read that?'

'It seems to be what happens in all the love stories I've read.'

'Dear Jane,' he was laughing she saw, 'move over——'

'Why?'

'Because I'm going to join you, not to kiss you and make you *melt*,' he said gravely despite the laughter still in his eyes, 'but because I think there is a crazy kind of love between us and perhaps we could console each other for a while.'

She moved and he lay down beside her, pushed some cushions behind their heads and put his arm beneath her shoulders. 'Comfortable?' he asked.

'Mmm.' She laid her cheek on his shoulder. 'Do you mean, console each other in a close but platonic way?'

'Something like that.' He stroked her hair.

'Two people with all sorts of problems but who understand each other better now? That kind of crazy love? Friends, in other words.'

'Yes. Relax.'

'I'm not very good at that,' she murmured, but in fact the warmth of his body was soothing her taut, over-wound nerves.

'Tell me more about your father. Where does he live?'

'Some place in Africa I've never heard of. He's going around Australia lecturing about it and trying to raise funds, then he's coming back to Brisbane. He's got green eyes, too.'

'And hair like midnight?' He slipped some strands through his fingers.

'No...' The word was blurred and indistinct and not long afterwards her tired, overburdened mind relinquished its hold and she fell asleep.

She woke in her bed, in her underwear, with no recollection of being undressed and put there. And she sat up abruptly, thinking of work, but remembered it was Saturday, changed into a nightgown and sank back into the warmth. To think of Liam...

As her thoughts roamed over all that had been said, she shivered though and realised why. If any man could be said to have a cynical view of love and marriage Liam had certainly expressed one last night, and after what he'd said about tough, independent women who didn't like to go down without a fight she'd been extremely foolish to believe that his cynicism hadn't coloured his view of women in general, and that he now found himself in the rather awkward position of having to disengage himself. Which was probably doing the right, the decent thing by his lights, but where did it leave her?

The faintest smile touched her lips. It would serve him right if I cast myself at his feet and went into a decline, she thought, it really would. But she sobered painfully and considered something else—the well-known fact that history had a habit of repeating itself. Children who'd been beaten by their parents often grew up into child beaters themselves, for example. Did, then, daughters who'd been abandoned by their fathers have an inclination to fall for men who would desert them? Surely not? she thought with another shiver. You'd think it would be the opposite, but...

She reached for the spare pillow and hugged it to herself. On the other hand, did I ever think he was falling in love with me as opposed to finding me a challenge? Not really, she admitted to the pillow. Except, well, the day he kissed me and said he'd like to give me some warmth and encouragement—what did he say? Something about it being what the best relationships are about... I think, she reflected, that really sparked this sense of curiosity. But now—she grimaced and buried her face in the pillow—now he's made it quite plain it's not on, so—where do I go from here?

'Hell!' She sat up and cast the pillow away in sudden disgust. 'I'm not and never could be the type that goes into a decline and I don't have to have things spelled out repeatedly, do I? No. So just watch your step, Liam Benedict. And I'm going to sleep in if it kills me...

It didn't, although it was a restless dream-laden sleep she fell into and when an almighty crash woke her out of it she wasn't sure if it was part of her dream or not.

But two seconds later a distinctly human groan of pain followed and she leapt out of bed and threw open her bedroom door to see Liam spreadeagled on his back on the living-room floor across the coffee-table, which had collapsed beneath him.

'Oh, my God,' she breathed and rushed over to him. 'Are you all right?' She pulled half the table away from him—he'd broken it in two—and knelt down beside him. 'What happened? Did you trip? Your back... You're very pale!' She twisted her hands together helplessly, resisting an urge to cradle them around his face, and stared down at him in horror. 'Can't you get up?'

'No, not at the moment,' he said with a grimace of pain, 'but——'

'But you could have half a coffee-table sticking into you!'

'I haven't—that's not the problem.'

'What is it, then?' She didn't realise she was as pale as he was and visibly trembling through her flimsy nightgown as if she were the one injured.

'It's my knee, gave way on me unexpectedly—look——'

'Your knee! I *told* you it wasn't a very satisfactory way of going about things, just waiting for it to collapse on you—really, for a grown man you're unbelievable, Liam Benedict! How on earth do you think I'm going to get you up? You need a crane...oh...'

'Jane,' he closed his hand around hers, 'calm down.' He waited a moment as she took a gulping breath and blushed.

'Sorry,' she muttered. 'Tell me what to do.'

'Bring over a couple of kitchen chairs; I can use them to lean on on the way up.'

She rushed to obey but it was five agonising minutes before he managed to get himself on to the settee and all she could do was flutter around uselessly. And when he did finally sink on to the settee, he was drenched in sweat and even paler.

'Your doctor,' she said. 'I'll ring him—and Sam!'

'Don't worry about Sam.'

'But we need someone to help move you, now don't argue!' she commanded forcefully although as she picked up the phone her fingers were rather useless, but she finally got through and the doctor said he would be round straight away. There was no reply from Sam's number.

Liam was lying with his eyes closed and his jaw rigid with pain as she came back to the settee. She put out a hand and touched his hair. 'Is there anything I can do?' she whispered.

'No.'

'He said he'd be here in minutes.'

His eyes flickered open and for a moment there was the old flicker of amusement in them as he said, 'You'd better put some clothes on, then.'

She looked down at herself and grimaced. 'All right. I'm sorry I shouted at you, I just got an awful fright. I thought you could have broken your back.'

'I'm not sure I haven't—no, just kidding. As a matter of fact, if you could keep doing that, it helps.'

She looked down at her fingers on his hair, stroking gently. 'This?'

'Mmm...'

'Well, it doesn't seem very much, nor would I want it to give you the wrong impression——' She stopped and bit her lip.

'What would that be?' His eyes were closed again.

'I . . . well, I wouldn't want you to think, for example, that I was trying to take up where I left off yesterday,' she finished in a rush. 'I mean, I do understand that there's no future for us, not that you can see anyway . . .' She broke off awkwardly, then said as prosaically as she was able, 'In other words, I'm just being platonic because I don't have to have things rammed home to me, you know.'

'Don't you? That's a pity,' he said barely audibly, 'because what would help me most just now, I think, would be to have you in my arms in a most unplatonic way. It might just conquer everything else . . .'

Jane stopped stroking and stared down at him with her lips parted. And she started to say something about how irrational that was—when she realised he'd blacked out.

'Oh, *God*!' She knelt down beside him and started to shake him again, from a helpless feeling of fear for him and an equally helpless feeling that was possibly as unplatonic as feelings could be. A desire to hold him and comfort him that caused her nipples to harden and a wave of tenderness to suffuse her body, taking her so much by surprise that she could only stare down at him transfixedly.

That was how the doctor found her, but with her hand on his hair again and her cheek on his shoulder.

'Well, Miss Mathieson, we'll be operating on Monday to repair the damage—we had hoped it would be unnecessary but it obviously isn't. Now, the big problem is not so much the operation but keeping him off that leg for at least six weeks afterwards, but I guess that's not your problem——'

'I do live in the same house with him—do you mean he has to stay in *bed* for six weeks?'

'Oh, no, he'll be able to get around on crutches, but the less pressure there is on the leg, the better, and there's not a lot one can do that way.'

'I see,' Jane said thoughtfully.

'Of course he has a lot of friends, I'm sure they'll all buck in and help, but at least one person living there will be a great help to him, won't it?'

Jane gazed at him then agreed belatedly as she wondered at the same time how it would help her. But to leave Liam Benedict in these circumstances seemed rather a mean and petty thing to do. Although, she mused drily, she could probably walk out into the street and in a matter of minutes find six girls who would throw up everything to take her place. 'Can I see him now?' she asked suddenly.

'By all means. I've given him something for the pain but he should be quite lucid.'

He was, although still pale and tired-looking.

Jane stood at the door of his private ward for a moment before he realised she was there, and waited to see if it happened to her again—the acute physical manifestations of her state of mind, a phenomenon she hadn't really believed in. It was no comfort to her that, to a lesser degree, it did. And, of course, it set her on the defensive.

'They tell me you'll have to be off that leg as much as possible for six weeks,' she said briskly and walked towards the bed. 'We can do one of two things. I can go and you can get whoever you want to live in or I can stay and keep house, but what with work I won't be there a lot, so it wouldn't really be ideal——'

'Hello, Jane,' he said quietly.

She coloured faintly then said stiffly, 'How do you feel now?'

'Fine.'

She raised an eyebrow. 'You don't look it. But to get back——'

'Sit down. You don't look too fine yourself.' He studied her pensively.

She opened her mouth, closed it then said with some asperity, 'Must be something to do with the unusual way I've spent this Saturday.'

'I'm sorry I gave you such a fright.'

She shrugged. 'It wasn't your fault, but we ought to sort things out now, don't you agree?' She eyed him sternly.

'It's up to you.'

Jane gritted her teeth while he merely watched and waited.

Then he said, 'Has it—this state you're in—anything to do with what I said just before I passed out?'

'I'm not in a state,' she denied.

'What *was* your reaction to what I said, then?' he queried, and neither the pain-killers nor his tiredness disguised the familiar glint of irony in his eyes, so blue against his *un*familiar pallor.

'I don't think this is the time or place to go into that, Liam,' Jane said with an effort, 'although I have to admit that in the light of what you said to me the night before, it was, well, a bit incredible, but I suppose men will be men and I for one obviously don't understand them very well——' She stopped abruptly.

'It was a spontaneous reaction; sorry,' he murmured, the irony replaced by a glint of amusement. 'So, you're right, we can do one of two things—put it down to a set of very unusual circumstances and ignore it, or,' the glance he shot at her was quite unfairly penetrating for someone in his condition, she thought hotly, 'we could——'

Jane stood up. 'No, look,' she broke in, 'we're not going to do anything of the sort. We've had this all out and I'm sick to death of it anyway!' She took a breath. 'All right, I'll stay just for the time being and because I feel I owe you some help but that's all.'

'You don't owe me anything, Jane,' he said slowly, and, for once, quite soberly. 'I'm the one with the unclear conscience...' He closed his eyes rather suddenly.

'Did...?' Jane stopped and bit her lip on the question that was uppermost in her mind—had he regained any consciousness before the doctor arrived? Because if he had he would know some things she desperately didn't want him to know. 'Do you want anything?' she said hurriedly. 'Books?'

'Thanks. Will you be all right on your own?' His lashes lifted.

'Of course,' she lied. 'I'm used to it.'

He was in hospital for a week.

Jane visited him twice then decided he had more than enough visitors—one had to virtually fight one's way in—and for the first few weeks of his convalescence at home it was the same. All she really did was provide food and keep house, and Sam stayed with them until Liam had got the hang of his crutches, but, anyway, she was tense not only because of her personal dilemma but because it was a strain having people popping in all the time, and he seemed oddly withdrawn, with her at least. She also thought she was the only one, apart from Sam perhaps, who realised he was still in a lot of pain, and it hurt her to have to watch him coping with his crutches and see him leaning against a wall with his eyes closed and sweat on his brow and know that to try to help him would only be futile and place the kind of strain on her defences she couldn't afford. Also to know that he didn't seem to want her help. As it was she'd just managed to stop herself several times from standing up and shouting to everyone to leave him alone with her. And that led her sometimes, when she couldn't censure her thoughts, to picture what it would be like to be married to him, to have him to herself to be able to love and cherish and talk to about anything under the sun, to do things together, to see if, as she had the feeling, a softer, sweeter Jane Mathieson might not emerge...

But, inevitably, one evening they did find themselves alone. She got home from work and put her briefcase and a bulging shopping bag down on the kitchen table, where he was sitting, with a sigh, as she looked around.

'You've been deserted,' she said lightly.

'Yes, thank God.'

'Weren't you enjoying all the attention?' She released her hair from its knot and kicked off her shoes.

He shrugged. 'It helped pass the time.'

'Feeling OK?' she asked, not too searchingly, she hoped, after a moment.

'No.'

'What's wrong?' This time she didn't try to hide her concern.

He lay back in his chair. 'What do you think, Jane?'

'I...' She looked at him then away, for there'd been an oddly insolent note in his voice. 'I would guess you're sick of these four walls, sick of your crutches, sick of the pain, but it's only a few weeks to go—and I've got something special for dinner tonight. I'll just go and change.'

She went and wondered why she seemed to be trembling inwardly, why she had the conviction there was some sort of a showdown in the air. And when she'd changed into jeans and a yellow sweater she was curiously reluctant, she discovered, to go back into the kitchen.

He was standing up when she reappeared, leaning against the sink with one crutch supporting his bad leg.

'Hungry?' she said brightly, and started to unpack the shopping bag.

He didn't answer as she piled some apples and oranges into the fruit bowl on the table and carefully unwrapped her special dinner: some fillets of his favourite fish that she was going to grill, make chips for, and the ingredients for a salad. She'd also bought a carton of minestrone soup to heat up and an apple pie for dessert.

She passed him twice as she carried things from the kitchen table and was going back for the apple pie when he put out a hand and closed it round her wrist. She stopped, side on to him, with her heart beating suddenly like a tom-tom, then turned to face him nervously. 'What is it?' she whispered.

'This,' he said, still only holding her wrist but with his blue gaze flicking from her mouth to her breasts in an oddly heavy-lidded way. 'I must apologise, Jane,' he added and his lips twisted, 'because if this bloody leg hadn't happened to me, I might have been able to stick to my, admittedly belated, but nevertheless good intentions. As it is, I'm going around the bend stuck here with you, having to watch the way you always let your hair down when you get home, always kick off your shoes then you straighten your shoulders and become a good little housekeeper although you're tired and all wound up still from work. Having to watch the way you're like a polite zombie in the morning and knowing I could make you wake up so differently. Having to wonder if I *could* relax you and how you'd be when you're languid with love. Sweet? I don't know, but, God help me, I'd like to try... Funny—yes, but perhaps always with that touch of tartness that makes you unique. That's what's wrong.'

Her lips parted but no sound came other than her jerky breathing and his gaze moved back to her breasts rising and falling beneath the yellow wool. 'Dying to undress you properly,' he said barely audibly, 'and run my hands up and down your beautiful body.'

'Liam ... Liam ...' Her voice broke. 'You were the one——'

'For my sins, do you think I don't *know* that?' he said harshly. 'It doesn't change this.' He pulled her closer so that their bodies were touching.

Once again shock held her rigid and stunned. 'But ... no, it couldn't work. When you're better you'll feel differently; this is only——'

'Forget about that—what about you?' he shot at her.

'What about m-me?' she stammered.

'Have things changed since you cried into my shoulder thinking I was out like a light and asked, "God, why him? Why had I to fall in love with him of all people?"'

'You heard!' A burning flush travelled up from the base of her throat. 'Were you ... were you faking?'

'No.' He smiled slightly. 'In fact I thought I might have dreamt it. Now I know I didn't.' He released her wrist and touched her hot cheek.

She bit her lip. 'You tricked me,' she accused in a low voice.

'Does it matter?'

She was silent, trying to gather her wits, trying to be unaffected by the feel of him, that look in his eyes. 'Yes, it matters,' she said raggedly at last, 'in the context that you didn't want me to fall in love with you, so——'

'Jane, there's one solution. It seems to me that the answer is for us to get married.'

CHAPTER EIGHT

JANE closed her eyes then opened them experimentally and whispered, 'Could you say that again?'

Liam smiled but not amusedly and said deliberately, 'Will you marry me, Jane?'

'Marry you,' she repeated, and licked her lips. 'Why?'

'Because I think it's what we both need.'

She gazed at him and found that her voice was stuck in her throat. Then she turned away and drew a deep breath and turned back. 'No, you don't,' she said huskily. 'You think it's what *I* need and you probably feel you have to take the responsibility for how I feel, but you don't. It would be a recipe for utter disaster in my mind. I just can't believe after all you've *said*——'

'Perhaps in all we've said,' he broke in, 'we've missed the one vital point. And it might be more important than words anyway—this.' He pulled her into his arms and his crutch clattered to the floor.

'Liam,' she breathed, staring up into his eyes with a kind of desperation, but his hand slid into her hair and he bent her backwards slightly and lowered his lips to hers.

Being kissed the way he kissed her then, slowly and with infinite patience, the way he moved his hand on her back and slid it gently beneath her jumper, was an experience so new and so incredibly sensual for Jane that she was powerless to resist. Her body would not respond to her mind which at first was flashing confused danger signals, or to anything but the mesmerising feel of his fingers on her skin, in the small of her back. And her mind had no control over the discovery that she wanted to press her breasts against the hard wall of his chest and her hips to his, and when he slid the fingers of his other hand down her throat she parted her lips helplessly and a tingling, liquid sensation ran through her body, a feeling of such expectancy that to contemplate it not being fulfilled was so devastating that she made a desolate, husky little sound and pressed herself even closer, unable to bear the thought of being parted from him, wanting to drown herself in Liam Benedict and this astonishing rapture.

He kissed her deeply then, and when it ended she was so stunned that she lay against him trembling as he propped himself back against the counter, holding him herself now about the waist, curving her body into his.

'For a girl who was worried about being able to *melt*, you do it beautifully, Jane,' he said barely audibly at last, and stroked her hair.

A bubble of laughter rose to her lips and she tipped her face up to his. 'I think you have to take the credit for it—so they were right,' she said ruefully.

'All those love stories you read?'

'Mmm. Well,' she lowered her eyes and sighed a shuddering little sigh, suddenly, 'it's still no reason to want to marry me.'

'It's one of the best.'

'No, I mean, as two people who *know* it isn't enough on its own, you from your own experience and me from my parents' experience——'

'My experience was a long time ago, Jane.' He put his hands about her waist and moved her away from him. 'This is something new. You said to me once that you were possessed of a curiosity about me.' He stopped and his gaze roamed over her in a way that seemed to dispense with her clothes and take possession of her body, even claim ownership of it, but not only that, in a way that made her feel weak and shaken and willing to submit not only her body but her innermost self to anything he cared to do with her, to his unspoken but implicit curiosity.

Why this man? she wondered agonisedly and not originally. Why do I feel as if I'm bound to him and can never escape whatever happens? Is it the way he laughs at me yet seems to *know* me better than anyone? What could it be for him? Assuming he does feel the same way...

'Jane?'

But in a flurry of confusion she leant back against him and half buried her face. 'I don't know what to say,' she whispered. 'Don't forget I am a lawyer. So I have to try to rationalise things and they just...won't rationalise!'

'You could try leaving it to me. It could also be that these things just don't respond to rationalisation. Perhaps they exist on a different plane.'

'I doubt if I could ever leave it all to you. I'm not that kind of person. And that's one thing——' she tilted her head back again to look into his eyes but her hair had fallen in hers and he brushed it away gently '—thanks—that would make it incredibly hard for us—apart from all the other things! We're such opposites. And I think I would always worry that you felt you had to marry me; I couldn't help it. I'm like that——'

'Jane,' he interrupted grimly, 'will you shut up or do I have to kiss you again to make you?'

A spark of anger lit her eyes. 'Then there's the fact that you're unbelievably dictatorial. I'm not used to that. I'm——'

'Yes, I am,' he said with a lazy glint in his eyes that gave her no warning of his intentions, which were to do exactly what he'd warned her of.

'Liam,' she protested, but that was the last word she got to say because he kissed her thoroughly and not particularly gently, and even managed to turn her indignation into an oddly motivated desire to give him back as good as he gave so that when they separated this time they were both breathing heavily and there was a current of electrical awareness running between them that made her stagger, and she would have fallen had he not pulled her back almost against him—he was still having to use the counter as a prop.

They stared at each other in silence for a long minute as Jane ran her tongue over her bruised mouth in amazement but couldn't, for the life of her, find a word to say nor a thing to do to ease the crackling, desperately physical tension between them. The kind of tension that had every nerve-ending in her body conscious of nothing but him and the way he was looking at her which let her know exactly what he'd like to do to her next. Her own confused inclination not to resist but not to go down without a fight either...

It was when she realised this that she closed her eyes suddenly and swayed in his arms, and, with an inaudible curse, he gathered her close, and said roughly, 'Jane, relax. You don't have to fight everyone or everything. You don't even have to fight yourself.'

Tears pricked her eyelids as she buried her face against him again, but, curiously, a lot of the fight had gone out of her and she made no move when he pushed both hands beneath her yellow sweater and caressed her shoulder-blades and under her arms. And against all her better judgement, she couldn't help but feel comforted as he rubbed his cheek against the top of her hair.

She never knew later how she, both of them for that matter, could have been so deaf, but her first intimation that they were not alone came when she felt Liam tense against her and felt him raise his head.

Then, to her horror, she heard him drawl over the top of her head, although he didn't withdraw his hands from under her jumper, 'Well, Brother James, this *is* a surprise.'

She froze and there was a crashing silence then Liam unhurriedly withdrew his hands and smoothed her jumper down. 'You must be Amanda. Welcome home. I'm Liam,' he added, and released Jane but took her hand and turned her away from him.

If Jane could have fallen through the floor she would have been eternally grateful. As it was she felt as if she was blushing from head to toe, but there was a squeak of pure joy and Amanda launched herself before their eyes even met.

'Oh, Jane. Jane!' she cried, and, upon reaching Jane, enveloped her in her arms and appeared to be laughing and crying at the same time. 'Oh, darling,' she went on, her words almost falling over each other in the way she had when she was moved or excited, 'I felt so guilty about you although James said I wasn't to, he was sure you understood, but I did even so and now...well, it's all worked out for the best for *both* of us. Oh, there's only one thing I regret—that we couldn't have had a double wedding!'

Twenty minutes later they were seated in the lounge, James was making coffee and Amanda was still talking nineteen to the dozen although they'd all ignored her reference to weddings, double or otherwise. Liam was sprawled out on the settee where his brother, on hearing the reason for the crutch and the fact that he was limping heavily, had consigned him, and his expression was entirely enigmatic as he responded to his sister-in-law's chatter. Of them all, only Jane had barely said a word.

And it was only the sudden frown that came to Amanda's eyes that prompted her to lift herself out of the daze she was in and say, 'It's lovely to see you, but we weren't expecting you home for months.'

Amanda glanced at James across the room and they exchanged a look of such open tenderness that Jane caught her breath.

'Well,' Amanda said with palpable pride, 'we hadn't planned on it yet, but I'm pregnant. And being pregnant and travelling doesn't seem to agree with me so we came home. But tell me,' the frown came back to her eyes as she glanced from Jane to Liam, 'you are both serious about each other, aren't you?'

James cleared his throat and shot his wife a warning glance. To which she replied with dignity and as if she were twice Jane's age and responsible for her into the bargain, 'If you knew Jane as I do, James, you would understand that she'd have to be very serious about a man to...to...well, you know what I mean.'

Jane winced inwardly and put her hands to her face and they stayed there arrested as Liam spoke.

'I'm very serious about Jane, Amanda,' he said placidly. 'In fact I was just asking her to marry me when you—interrupted us.'

It was perhaps fortunate that Amanda didn't see James nearly drop the sugar bowl, and unfortunate that Jane did, through her fingers.

Amanda in fact looked immensely gratified but it seemed she still had a problem on her mind. 'I must say,' she ventured candidly, 'much as I like you so far and from what James has told me, I wouldn't have thought you'd appeal to Jane somehow.' Her brow creased again.

Jane dropped her hands into her lap and swallowed but her voice just wouldn't work.

'I didn't, not at first,' Liam said lazily, and, in exercise of that compelling power he had over her, forced her to look up and across at him; to witness the tiny glint of irony in his blue gaze? she wondered as he went on, 'It would be safe to say that she took an instant dislike to me but there were reasons for that. Once we got to know each other better, though, she,' his lips twisted, 'not without some reluctance and some coaxing—changed her mind. Your sister is a very fiery lady, Amanda, as I suppose you know. So it's just as well I'm more even-tempered and very difficult to best in a fight and that I understand her so well.'

Jane actually shuddered as Liam Benedict delivered himself of this masterpiece and her own sister actually gave a decisive nod of approval—she's dumber than I ever gave credit for, she thought without a pang—but what Amanda said then capped it all.

She said, 'Then you have my blessing. I always knew Jane needed someone stronger and not afraid of her. I just didn't see how *she* could be convinced of it. But that's love, I guess.'

At last Jane found herself able to speak although with difficulty. 'Darling, you've only been married a couple of months but you seem to be setting yourself up as an authority.'

Amanda grinned. 'I may not be an authority on marriage but I am an authority on *you*. Don't forget I've known you all my life. And for a long time now I've thought that whoever you fell in love with would have to be someone strong enough to take no nonsense from you. Only *you* couldn't see it.'

Jane lay fully clothed on her bed much later and wondered if that was the definitive summing up of her, those words spoken by her own sister—words out of the mouths of babes? 'Or one of those uncannily intuitive people who are not at all dumb, God forgive me.'

She sighed deeply then stiffened as she heard the unmistakable sound of Liam on his crutch outside her door. To all intents and purposes, the rest of the evening had been a happy time. She and Amanda had done a loaves and fishes act with dinner, and Amanda and James had regaled them with the highlights of their trip and Amanda had been delighted to hear her baby would have a grandfather. Then she'd wilted suddenly and James had taken her to bed, and Jane had taken the opportunity to do the same, stoically disregarding Liam's quizzical look as she'd left the lounge with a simple goodnight.

'What does he expect?' she'd muttered to herself as she'd closed her bedroom door. 'That I'd be a willing party to this *charade*? That I'd be happy to be dissected and discussed as if I were a backward child?'

But as her bedroom door opened and Liam limped in, switching on the light, a feeling of strange powerlessness came over her, and she only moved her cheek on the pillow then regarded him bleakly as he closed the door and sat down in the armchair.

'Come to check on the reluctant bride?' she said after a moment.

He moved his shoulders but his expression of almost clinical interest—Damn him, she thought—didn't change. 'How do you feel, Jane?' he queried quietly.

She thought for a moment then laughed. 'How do I feel? Like the remains of a leg of roast lamb, actually. My mother had a close friend once and they used to spend hours discussing butchers et cetera, and whether the last leg they'd got wasn't actually mutton dressed up as lamb or whether they'd overcooked the thing or how dear it had been or how cheap but it had tasted all right although of course there'd been plenty of garlic used—that's how I feel. Curiously depleted as well as turned inside out, if you must know, Liam. So if we could take a rain check on this conversation, not to mention all the events that have led up to it, I'd really appreciate it.'

'So that you can lie here and torment yourself?' he said thoughtfully.

'If that's an oblique offer to lie here with me, no thanks——'

'Watch your step, Jane,' he warned on a suddenly harsh, impatient note.

She sat up. 'Don't threaten me, Liam, and don't think you can use physical blackmail on me—nothing, *nothing*,' she repeated, 'can alter the fact that you've treated me like a complete fool tonight or that you've grossly misrepresented things to my own sister not to mention your own brother, who incidentally kept *looking* at you as if to say, "I don't believe this"... Why would he look like that, Liam? Could it be that he knows you well enough to know that the wedded state is not exactly your highest ideal?'

'If you'll allow me to take your speech—I did tell you once you really should be at the bar, didn't I?—well I'll amend that,' he said dispassionately. 'Your delivery is excellent but your logic leaves a lot to be desired—if I can take your speech one point at a time, I don't think it was any misrepresentation to tell Amanda that I'd just asked you to marry me, nor to tell her that I thought I'd be good for you—or something to that effect——'

'Something to that effect,' Jane said incredulously. 'You . . . she . . . you *agreed* that I need a strong man who would stand no nonsense from me. Have you no idea how humiliating not to mention *archaic* that sounds——?'

'Would you rather I'd told her you're dying to go to bed with me, Jane? You certainly kissed me as if you were, you've told me as much; and because *I* can't walk away from *you*, my dear, I suggested the only possible solution for us.'

'No,' she whispered, her strength giving out suddenly. 'It's a solution but not the right one. I may have a lot of faults, Liam, I may even be downright stupid, but I think if I did marry anyone I'd want to believe I was *loved*. Not just rescued from the consequences of what you believe was an indiscretion on your part or perhaps even a crusading desire to deal with your guilt about your first marriage.'

They stared at each other. 'That's a new one,' he drawled finally. 'Did you think it up on the spur of the moment?'

Jane closed her eyes. 'In lieu of being able to tell me you love me madly, mightn't it have some foundation?'

'You forget,' he said coolly, 'that it's your father who has the crusading spirit, not me. But I can tell you that I want you—rather badly. However, I too don't have to have things rammed home to me, Jane. Shall we call it quits?' His eyes held hers and didn't miss the sudden spark of confusion in them. 'I'll explain to Amanda if you like.'

'Call it all off?' she said slowly and unwisely.

'Are you offering me an affair, Jane?'

She coloured and breathed exasperatedly. 'I . . . no. I . . . you just go a bit too fast for me sometimes, Liam.'

'Then what *do* you want me to do, Jane?'

Their eyes clashed again. 'Tell me the truth,' she said hoarsely.

'The truth?' he said quite gently. 'I do worry about you, Jane. That might not be the same thing as declaring mad passionate love to you but I also admire you.' He smiled slightly as her eyes widened. 'In fact I admire your fighting spirit very much and it occurred to me that you might never bore me and that *these* things could be more sane and enduring and they could be built upon better than a flush of overheated, sentimental claptrap—do you think if your father had made a sane rational decision he would have married your mother?'

'That's hitting below the belt,' she said starkly.

'Well, tell me what you think,' he persisted.

Jane didn't say anything for a long time. Then she got up and wandered over to the window. 'I can't help wondering,' she said desolately, 'whether while you're being so sane and rational I'll be making a fool of myself.'

'If you came here, I'd be able to show you otherwise.'

'If I did that, I'd be giving in to something I don't believe in.' She turned towards him and her face was pale and weary.

He grimaced. 'You can't have it both ways, Jane. What do you believe in? The passion or the logic?'

She winced.

'On the other hand, if you believed in a bit of both, we'd really have a common purpose—a rationalised decision which you seem to hold dear to your heart, and a physical need for each other that's quite in tune with the state of wedlock. Tell me, have you ever visualised what it would be like to be married to me?'

She was too late to still the protesting little sound she made in her throat and it was a dead giveaway, as his eyes told her, not mockingly but in an unmistakable acknowledgement and so that she felt, at last, that she had no place to hide, no defences left. Although she made one last-ditch effort. 'I couldn't live with the thought that you felt *sorry* for me.'

'Then I'll make you a promise,' he said steadily. 'If I ever feel sorry for you, I'll tell you. Come here, Jane.'

'Liam——'

'How you can imagine I'll ever feel sorry for you when you intend to fight me to the bitter end I don't know. I'm the one in need of sympathy if anything.' His eyes glinted with a spark of amusement.

'No, you're not!' she retorted with an uprush of spirit as she saw that glint. 'You're the one who thinks you can call all the shots—for reasons I've yet to understand—and you're the one who can play hot and cold, can lecture me, can *tell* me you're so cynical about marriage and that it's not on your agenda and shouldn't be on mine, not with you and then . . . and then . . . is it any wonder I'm confused?' she finished, then glanced at the door anxiously.

'I doubt if you'll wake them,' Liam murmured and grimaced. 'They're not only sleeping the sleep of the exhausted—it was a thirteen-hour flight—but the sleep of the righteous married couple. If there's one thing about marriage that doesn't appeal to me,' he continued reflectively, 'it's that essentially smug air it gives some who come to it. Is that what you meant when you accused your sister of setting herself up as an authority?'

'Yes,' Jane said shortly.

'Then we'll have to try to restrain ourselves, won't we, when it comes to us?'

Jane stared at him and said involuntarily, 'Liam, do you realise you're like a human steam-roller?'

He smiled and simply held his hand out to her, and she went weak inside, and knew that not to take it was to condemn herself to a cold loneliness she didn't know if she could bear.

She licked her lips. 'I don't want to sleep with you tonight,' she said hoarsely.

'You did earlier. Want to.'

She coloured. 'I know. But I don't think it's right to make that kind of decision now.'

'Are you saying you'll only come to be kissed and consoled?' His blue gaze swept lazily over her.

'It might sound a little ridiculous,' she said carefully then her shoulders sagged, 'but yes. And that might not be fair to you, so——'

'If you think it will also leave your options open, Jane, you're wrong, but be that as it may—I'm actually not capable at the moment.'

Her eyes widened. 'Capable of what?' she said foolishly.

His eyes laughed at her. 'Making love to you. Once I'm flat on my back, any unwise movement of my leg causes me considerable pain still. It'll be a couple of weeks yet before you'll have to make that decision.'

Jane snorted. 'You might have told me——'

'Sorry. I didn't realise it was a matter of *such* urgency with you——'

'I don't mean that! I've just told you I *didn't* want to...oh!' she breathed angrily as she saw the wickedly grave way he was regarding her. 'I hate you sometimes, Liam.'

'I know,' he said softly.

'Perhaps I'm not as much in love with you as you seem to think—I gather you *do* think that now. Well, maybe you're wrong!'

'I can see I'll have to come to you——'

'No! No,' she said hastily as he made to rise and she saw his hands whiten on the arms of the chair. Then she realised there were tears running down her cheeks and she sat down on the bed and scrubbed her face furiously—and he got up and came over to the bed and stood over, staring down at her sombrely.

'Jane?' he said at last.

She looked up, with new tears welling.

'All you have to do is say yes. I promise you, I'll take care of the rest.' He stared down at her for a moment longer then eased himself down beside her but only took her hand in his.

'You must have great faith in yourself, Liam—or something.'

'In fact, I have rather a lot of faith in you.'

She smiled wryly through her tears. 'Because I don't *melt* too badly, after all?'

He slid his fingers through hers but said no more.

She sighed suddenly and laid her head on his arm. 'All right. I mean,' she amended hastily, 'we can get engaged.'

'Provided you don't want to be engaged for months.'

'Well...'

'One month should do it,' he said. 'Don't forget we've been living together for a couple of months.' She didn't see the wicked little glint in his eye but knew it was there all the same.

'Are you issuing an ultimatum, Liam?' she responded a shade tartly.

'I'm pointing out to you that we already know each other's likes and dislikes, habits and so on and don't seem to have any problems in that regard.'

Jane brooded for a moment but had to admit he was right. 'Still...' she temporised.

'One month, Jane,' he said mildly, but she knew he meant it. 'I presume you view an engagement as an escape clause in true legal style, but that's as long as it needs to be.'

She coloured and bit her lip and thought of telling him that if anyone might need an escape clause it was him, but she had the distinct feeling it would be like knocking her head against a brick wall so she remained silent.

'The other thing is,' he said after a time, 'living with James and Amanda for too long would prove a bit much for me, I'm sure.'

Jane had to smile and she said without thinking, 'Where *would* we live?'

'As a matter of fact I've just bought a town house in Spring Hill—as an investment—but if you liked it we could live there.'

Jane sat up and felt a little tremor of excitement. Spring Hill was exactly where she'd choose to live if she had a choice. Close to the city yet with a village air, views and open spaces. 'I would like that——' She stopped self-consciously.

His lips twisted wryly but all he said was, 'Good. We'll go and see it tomorrow. I think I'd like to meet your father too, before we get married. Can you get in touch with him?'

'Yes. He's due back in Brisbane in a couple of days.'

'Then there's only one thing left to say—tonight.'

'What's that?' She looked up at him enquiringly.

'Actually, I'd rather show you,' he said gravely, 'and let it speak for itself. But then again, a few words mightn't go amiss. It's going to be a long few weeks.' He put his fingers beneath her chin and stroked the soft skin very lightly. 'It's already been—a long time since you crashed through the window, Jane, and fell into my arms.'

She shivered with pleasure at his touch but said, 'That wasn't exactly how it happened.' Then, 'Haven't you had a——?' She stopped and blushed.

'A woman? Not since that night, no.'

'Oh,' she said softly, and lifted her face to his, and it was impossible to hide the impact this had made on her.

'I thought you might approve,' he observed seriously but with his eyes glinting. 'Any further objections?'

Jane considered. 'I'm thinking.'

He laughed outright and drew her into his arms. 'Why don't you think about this for a change?' He kissed her lightly and cupped her breast.

She sighed and slipped her arms around his neck. 'I must say it does feel—very right.'

CHAPTER NINE

BEING engaged was of course an entirely new experience for Jane in spite of having lived in the same house as Liam for some time.

Being engaged meant being kissed and touched a lot whenever James and Amanda weren't present—she didn't feel quite happy about it when they were, which Liam seemed to understand although he did look at her with a funny little glint in his eye sometimes. James and Amanda had no such inhibitions.

But there was also the time when her inhibitions took wings, such as the day they decided to drive down to the Gold Coast to celebrate his being given the go-ahead to drive his car again, which luckily was an automatic. But they got no further than halfway down the Pacific Highway when a police car with a flashing blue light and a wailing siren passed them at speed then an ambulance and they realised from the way the traffic was slowing and banking up that there must be an accident ahead.

Jane grimaced then noticed that Liam's hands were white about the steering-wheel and he was looking ahead rather fixedly. 'What...? Oh,' she said on a breath, 'look, turn off up there, we could go to Jacob's Well instead of the coast!'

He turned off and drove for about a mile through deserted, browsing countryside in dead silence. Then he pulled off the road beside a grassy paddock without a word.

Jane put her hand on his arm. 'Are you all right?'

He turned to her and she saw that he also had sweat trickling down his face, and said bitterly, 'I feel an awful fool.'

'Oh, Liam,' she said softly, 'no, you're not. You're only human.'

He pulled her into his arms and buried his face in her hair. But although it started out as just some kind of human contact he seemed to desperately need, it soon changed and they were kissing deeply and his exploration of her body beneath her clothes was becoming more and more intimate.

As for her, the confines of the car, the deserted road, everything seemed to melt away as she drowned in the wonder of his touch that turned her into a creature helpless with desire, the wonder of being able to touch in return as well as the feeling of being needed.

And so, when someone tapped on the roof, it took a long moment for her to come back to earth, then to turn away convulsively as she realised there was a man standing at Liam's window, grinning widely.

He was a strawberry farmer, he explained obligingly, and although they obviously didn't realise it they were parked across the gate that led to his strawberries and he couldn't get his tractor through. He'd waited a while, he added, but time was getting on and where strawberry plants that needed watering were concerned time was money.

Jane didn't follow the rest of the conversation—she was too busy trying to discreetly readjust her cardigan and blouse—but after what seemed like an age but was only a minute or so Liam started the car, moved it well out of the gate's way, stopped it again and waved the strawberry farmer through.

'How—embarrassing,' she said, but couldn't help chuckling suddenly.

'Sorry.' He turned to her and grinned and laid his arm along the back of the seat then let his hand drift down to arrest what she was doing to her clothes. 'We seem to make a habit of this. Don't.' He flicked a few buttons undone. 'It's quite safe now.'

'Well...' she temporised.

'And I rather enjoy seeing how you look after—we'd have to call that a fairly heavy necking session, wouldn't we? Something I haven't done since I was about Sam's age,' he said wryly.

'That's an awful term,' Jane protested.

'So long as you enjoyed it I don't mind what term we use,' he said softly.

Jane's mouth dimpled at the corners. 'I—enjoyed it,' she said ruefully. 'That much must have been patently obvious. It's when you give it names like that that it seems,' she wrinkled her nose, 'slightly wayward and wanton.'

His amused gaze dropped to her breasts, where her blouse was open again, but they were still covered by the satin and lace of her bra. He said barely audibly, 'The thought of you being wayward and wanton with me, Jane, is breathtaking.'

She smiled, a little uncertainly because, incredibly, despite her lingering embarrassment, she was still aroused, still amazingly affected by him, and it really didn't seem so awful to be caught "necking"—something she would have died rather than do before she met Liam Benedict. Her eyes widened at the thought.

All this must have been decipherable from her expression because his lips twisted and he sat forward and began to button her up himself. 'You're right,' he said gravely. 'We should really behave ourselves and conduct ourselves like adults.' He buttoned the last button, took her chin in his hand and kissed her lips gently. 'Thanks for understanding earlier. I thought I'd got over it all but for a few minutes there I was right back in it.'

She opened her mouth to offer to drive but closed it and kissed the inside of his wrist instead.

Being engaged involved a lot of talking, which she discovered, she was quite happy to do for hours, late into the night, and discovered herself even ringing him up from work impulsively—it could be said she took to being engaged like a duck to water, she reflected ruefully once.

And being engaged seemed to stifle a lot of her doubts although there were moments when it was a conscious effort to do it, she realised. Such as seeing the little flare of shock in Sam's eyes when he was told the news, and the way James on the odd occasion just couldn't hide the spark of speculation in his eyes.

Her ring, an emerald—Liam had said that with her eyes nothing else would be right—also caused Laura to be seriously astounded for the first time for years.

She noticed it immediately and dropped a stack of letters all over the floor. 'Jane! Am I dreaming or have you got yourself engaged?'

'You're not dreaming,' Jane replied a shade awkwardly.

'Who to?'

Jane grimaced. 'Who do you think?'

'Not Liam Benedict!'

'None other.'

'But I thought you were only being platonic—Jane! Tell me!' she begged.

'If you must know, he's a hard man to be platonic with.'

'Darling, *I* could have told you that, I didn't think you—but he's asked you to marry him?' Laura's eyes were still popping.

'I may be a lot of things,' Jane's patience was wearing thin, 'but you needn't carry on as if I were the last girl on earth he would marry,' she said tartly.

'I didn't mean that, well—of course I didn't mean *that*. It's just that he's resisted it for a long time, apparently.'

'I know,' Jane said a little bleakly.

'Oops—have I put my foot in my mouth?'

Jane shrugged then said briskly, 'No——'

'When's the wedding?'

'In a few weeks——' Fortunately her phone rang and saved her further embarrassment. In their next encounter, Laura merely enthused and insisted on taking her to her favourite boutique in their lunchtime.

Which caused Jane to say to Liam that night, 'This wedding——'

'Our wedding?'

'Of course. What other wedding would we be talking about?'

'I don't know. Your phrasing was slightly detached, that's all.'

Jane, who was actually lying in his arms on the settee, breathing in his heady essence and loving the way his hands were moving slowly on her body, reflected wryly that it was a miracle anything about her at all could remain detached. 'Our wedding, then,' she amended. 'What will it be like?'

He tilted her chin so he could look into her eyes. 'However you want it to be.'

'It's a bit close for too many trimmings but I did see a dress today, an outfit rather...' She broke off.

'Go on.' His eyes were amused.

'Well, that would suit a very quiet church wedding and perhaps a luncheon at a nice restaurant afterwards with a few friends—and family, of course.'

'Of course,' he agreed gravely, but added before she could take offence, 'That sounds ideal.'

She relaxed against him. 'If I organise the restaurant will you do the rector?'

'As a matter of fact I have a friend——'

'I might have known!'

'Yes, well—you'll like him although he'll probably insist on lecturing us on connubial bliss and how to maintain it, et cetera, et cetera.'

'Oh.' Jane was silent for a moment. 'Never let the sun go down on a quarrel—that kind of thing?'

'Mmm.' His hand rested lightly on her breast. 'Always sleep in a double bed.'

Jane grinned. 'We'll need a well-sprung one otherwise I'll keep rolling on to you.'

'That mightn't be a problem.'

And Jane had to concede rather ruefully that it mightn't. But she did say, 'How long will this last, do you think?'

'This what?'

'This.' A tinge of pink came to her cheeks. 'Feeling like this. I mean—well, to be honest, it's interfering with my work. I just wondered if, say, in twelve months' time, I'll still be finding it difficult to concentrate.'

'I'd like to think that could be the case in twelve years' time,' he said.

For some reason this made Jane feel slightly cross. 'I'm serious,' she said with dignity as an image of herself twelve years hence behaving like a love-sick schoolgirl filled her mind. While he, no doubt, would continue to be giving no outward manifestation—well, she amended, as his hands moved again, down to her hips, like this, yes, but he doesn't appear to be dreamy and forgetful at other times, he doesn't stop what he's saying and doing suddenly, can't even *remember* what he was saying or why he was doing whatever as I do, and simply stare at him and *then*, heaven help me, blush like a fool...

And just thinking of it made her feel hot suddenly and she tried to bury her face in his chest.

'Jane.' He slipped his fingers through her hair and waited until she looked up at last, and his lips twisted at her red cheeks. 'I'd say,' he said gently, 'that in twelve months' time "this" will have settled into something a little less hectic but just as nice.' And he bent his head and started to kiss her.

'Liam,' she said a long time later, 'do you...do you want to wait until we're married or... I mean...' She stopped awkwardly.

'Do you?'

'No,' she said honestly and grimaced, 'but then another part of me seems to say that would make it— extra-special. I don't know which one to listen to. You see, perhaps it mightn't *be* extra-special, I might be an awful failure, I might take months to get it right——'

'You won't,' he interrupted wryly.

'How can you tell?'

'You wouldn't be so happy doing this.'

'Oh.'

He tilted her chin and kissed the tip of her nose. 'Don't worry so much. By the way, I thought we might go out and choose some furniture tomorrow.'

Jane sat up with a sudden surge of excitement. She'd seen the town house and fallen in love with it. 'I'd love to! But,' she took a determined breath, 'I insist on helping to pay for it. After my mother died and we sold the house I became relatively wealthy, very relatively, but all the same.'

'Well, since we're being so traditional,' he said lazily, 'why don't you use your money to bring the kind of things brides used to bring to a marriage? Linen and that kind of stuff.'

'Oh,' Jane said again. 'Are you agreeing with the part of me that wants to be traditional, incidentally?'

He smiled at her. 'Yes. The thought of making it extra-special appeals to me somehow. Do you have any preference for a honeymoon?' he queried.

Jane considered then she said slowly, 'I think I'd like to spend the first night, anyway, in our... home. Would you mind?'

His fingers kept sliding through her hair. 'I like the sound of that a lot.'

'Why?' she whispered.

He grimaced. 'You ask a lot of questions—must be your legal mind. Er—it seems to show a commitment to this marriage, I guess. As if all those doubts you entertained are fading.'

'Well—oh, they are,' she confessed ruefully. 'I'm only surprised I haven't gone out and brought a stackful of bridal magazines.'

He laughed.

'Liam? What did you think of my father?' she asked. 'You seemed to be a bit reserved,' she said thoughtfully, thinking of the evening before, which had been nearly as bewildering as the first occasion her father had re-entered her life. Mainly on account of Amanda, she'd thought at the time, who was so very like her mother in looks. She'd seen it strike her father like a blow although Amanda apparently noticed nothing, had been her usual apparently unconscious self and had accepted this stranger back into her life as if it were the most natural thing in the world. But the more Jane thought of it, the more she realised that there had been a certain constraint between Liam and her father which had not been apparent with James.

'I guess,' Liam paused, 'it would be natural for him to have some reservations about me. Considering that you hadn't told him anything about me, had given him the impression that you were heart-whole and fancy free, in fact.'

'At the time, that was the way—it looked as if it would have to be,' Jane reminded him, a shade tartly.

But he disregarded it and went on, 'I suppose now he's found you again he might like more of your time, too. He——' again he paused '—kept looking at you as if he unearthed a gold nugget.'

'Did he?' Jane turned this over in her mind and felt a warm little glow. 'He is rather nice, isn't he?'

Liam didn't answer.

'You're not still worried that I'm looking for a father figure, are you?'

'No,' Liam said rather drily, she thought. 'I think he's looking for a daughter figure—I think you'll be hearing a lot more from him, Jane.'

Prophetic words, Jane was to discover. Her father had had one last part of Australia to visit, Cape York and Thursday Island, before he flew home to Africa, and it was a couple of days after she'd discussed him with Liam that he rang her up, told he was back in Brisbane and would like to spend his last day with her and Amanda. So Jane took the day off work, she and Amanda prepared a special lunch and James and Liam—who was going into the office now more and more—tactfully absented themselves for a lot of the day.

And it was while Amanda was taking an afternoon nap—pregnancy made her incredibly sleepy apparently—that Alex Mathieson suggested to his daughter Jane that she postpone her wedding and come to Africa for a few weeks with him.

'I...' Jane was making coffee and she looked across to where he was sitting on the settee she and Liam so often occupied. To see that he was deadly serious—in fact more than that. There was no mistaking the concern in his green eyes. 'I don't think Liam would appreciate that,' she said finally.

'Why not? Oh, I can understand that it must seem very odd me taking an interest after all these years, but——' He shrugged painfully.

'I've explained that to Liam. In fact he understands rather well. His first marriage was similar to yours and Mum's, although he hasn't lost touch with——' She stopped.

Her father closed his eyes and laid his head back wearily. 'If you've any idea how I want to make up for that, Jane.'

Jane poured the coffee and brought it over. And she said honestly after a moment, 'I can also understand how difficult it could have been when we were little but once I'd grown up, once I'd left school...' She looked at him, unable to mask the hurt in her eyes.

'It was guilt then,' Alex said very quietly. 'The thought that, even if she hadn't turned you completely against me both of you could never forgive me and I could hardly blame you. That's how you let things slide just a little longer, that's when you tell yourself, maybe it's better to let sleeping dogs lie. But when I discovered, belatedly unfortunately, that...your mother had died I knew I couldn't let things slide any longer.'

Jane grimaced. 'I thought that once too—about sleeping dogs.'

'Jane,' he sat up and picked up his cup, 'I know you probably feel I have no right to say this but not only do I...want to see more of you, as much as possible but I also want you to,' he hesitated, 'feel very sure before you marry Liam—marry *anyone*. I...and this marriage seems to have sprung up out of the blue, rather.'

'Don't you like him?' As she said it, she caught the echo of that similar conversation with Liam.

Her father looked perturbed. 'I don't dislike him, I don't really know him well enough to be forming cast-iron opinions, and on the surface he's—well, he gives the impression of integrity and so on yet, I just can't help feeling there's something...unusual between you. Is he the first man you've been in love with, Jane?'

'Yes.' She said it a little bleakly and wondered whether she should burden her father with the true story of her relationship with Liam, the story of her anachronistic state, but it occurred to her that he'd probably guessed that anyway. And instead she asked him a question, trying to sound light-hearted as she did so. 'You don't seem to be worried about Amanda like this.'

'I could be wrong, but those two are in their seventh heaven and not much will change it.'

'You could be right,' Jane agreed ruefully. 'But of course you and Mum must have had some seventh-heaven times.'

'Some,' he agreed. 'But if you must know, I started to panic about two weeks after the wedding.'

Jane winced.

He said sadly. 'We just didn't know each other well enough.'

'I know Liam pretty well,' Jane said and hoped her voice didn't lack conviction. 'Would you consider... being here for the wedding?'

Her father digested this. 'I would love to,' he said eventually. 'But two weeks is—if you could just give me a month. I *have* to leave tomorrow, I have commitments I can't get out of—but if not,' he said slowly, 'yes, I'll be here if I have to swim.' He smiled at her and held out his hand and she put hers into it and understood that he'd said his piece and that was all he would do, all he felt he had the right to do. But his perception of something unusual between her and Liam lingered with her after they all farewelled him the next morning.

Liam took her out to dinner that night. And said, 'You're quiet, Jane. Sad?'

'A bit,' she confessed. 'Liam,' she paused, 'tell me about Rory.'

'He's got red hair like his mother and my eyes, he's a rather studious kid and not at all into body contact sports, he's a bit shy and reserved—a lot like James in personality, actually,' he said wryly, 'but I spent as much time with him as I could during this last visit, we went trout fishing and stuff, and I think he enjoyed himself. He gets on really well with his stepfather, fortunately and,' he shrugged, 'appears to be coping pretty well all round.'

'Does he ever come over here to spend holidays with you?'

'He hasn't seemed to want to do that yet so I haven't
pushed it but I go over once a year at least, more if I
can, and he comes to stay with me.'

'So it can be done,' she said barely audibly.

'Jane,' he pushed aside some silverware and laid his
hand on hers, 'don't forget, Maureen, his mother, found
happiness with someone else.'

'Liam,' Jane took a deep breath, 'in the context of
feeling that two wrongs don't make a right, would you
agree to postpone the wedding for a month? So that my
father can come without...having to swim?' And she
explained to his suddenly raised eyebrow.

'Jane, no, I wouldn't—hang on, let me tell you why,'
he said drily as she tensed. 'I don't think your father's
commitments are the problem; I think he'd like you to
delay the wedding for other reasons. Now he's found
you he's not at all eager to let you go, he'd like to play
a bigger role in your life and help you to make your
decisions, probably both of you but it's a bit late for
Amanda—all of which is fairly natural, but to my mind
he gave away the right to do that years ago. So no,
although don't imagine I'll object to you getting to know
your father better, I won't, but *this* is just between us,
Jane. No one else. And that applies to when, how and
why we get married.'

She stared at him and shivered inwardly because there
it all was, in his cool blue gaze, the uncompromising set
of his mouth, the sheer size and strength of him as well
as his perception, his cleverness—all the things about
him, in fact, that he often lulled you into imagining
weren't there. But of course the better you got to know
Liam Benedict, the more you realised there was an iron
will beneath those easygoing ways. Have I allowed myself
to be more lulled than I realised? she wondered sud-

denly. Well, I couldn't be accused of giving in without
a fight but this... this is a bit like running into a brick
wall. Is this the consequence of not being *really* loved
and therefore understood? Even if he's right about my
father, surely he could understand how I feel?

'Well?'

She blinked and hoped the ridiculous tears she'd felt
pricking her eyelids weren't visible. 'Perhaps you're
right,' she murmured.

He picked up her hand and fiddled with her engagement ring. 'Why do I feel short-changed?' he said
with a faint smile. 'Because that's not your usual aggressive reaction to being crossed?'

She put her free hand to her mouth in an oddly helpless
little gesture because that hidden feeling in her heart that
it would be a mistake to marry Liam Benedict, the one
she'd been trying to bury, had even convinced herself
she had buried ever since the day James and Amanda
had arrived home and she'd agreed to it, was refusing
to stay hidden any longer. But how to handle it? she
wondered. Where did all my aggressive reactions ever
get me? They got me here, she answered herself, sitting
opposite him, wearing his engagement ring despite all
my doubts, loving him in a way I know he doesn't love
me. And *knowing* I could be as aggressive or shrewish
as I'm capable of without achieving a thing, without
being able to get across to him that what he feels for me
is not *love*; it's a compromise, part attraction, part a
sense of responsibility, perhaps still partly a challenge
but not the ultimate accord of two people deeply in
love... And, perhaps more to the point, a barrier drawn
across his deepest feelings that I can only dash myself
against in growing frustration—is that what Laura suspected and my father saw? Is that why James is still not

convinced although he tries to hide it and even Sam, despite his preoccupation with Elizabeth Green, is sort of restrained? It's only Amanda who really believes this can work... But how *can* I explain it to him?

Maybe you can only lay down your arms completely... She swallowed suddenly and tensed inwardly at what she was thinking then forced herself to relax. 'The furniture should have arrived today. Shall we go and have a look?'

'Ah,' he said as he unlocked the door of the town house and switched on a light that didn't work. 'One problem: the electricity isn't connected yet.'

'It doesn't matter,' Jane murmured. 'Look at the moon shining through the windows and anyway,' she glanced around, 'if the things I bought have been delivered—yes, they have—then I've got a surprise for you.'

Her surprise, after she'd delved through a package, was a set of two heavy crystal cubic candle holders and a box of cream candles. 'There,' she set them on the dining table, 'all I need is a match.'

'Here.' He handed her a pocket book of matches from the restaurant. 'I haven't smoked for years but I still collect matches.'

She lit the candles carefully and the shadows receded a little, showing up the new furniture. So far they'd only bought for the living and dining area and one bedroom but every piece had been chosen carefully and Jane looked around with tears in her heart but a determination to do what she had to do. 'Shall we go upstairs? Oh—we might as well take this up, it's linen. I'll carry the candles.'

She thought he glanced at her strangely but he picked up the two heavy parcels she'd indicated and followed her up the stairs into the main bedroom.

Their brand new double bed gleamed beneath the mixture of moonlight shining through the arched windows and candlelight, the mattress encased in plastic wrapping.

She put the candles down and glinted him a smile. 'Shall we have a dress rehearsal? I'm dying to see how the bedspread goes with the carpet.'

He lifted an eyebrow. 'If you like.'

'Well, you take off all the plastic and I'll open this.' She turned to the packages.

But it was quite a long moment before she heard him dealing with the plastic and once it was off she didn't look at him directly as she went about making the bed with the mushroom-pink sheets she'd chosen, putting pillowcases on the pillows and finally arranging the pewter and pink padded bedspread over it. 'Mmm. Looks nice, doesn't it? Tones well with the carpet.'

'Yes, it does.' He stared at her for a moment then sat down on the bed. 'Jane, what are you doing?'

She turned away from the frown in his eyes and walked over to the window where she took several deep breaths before turning back.

'This, Liam,' she said very quietly and raised her hands to release her hair. 'Please stay there,' she added, as he moved abruptly. 'I know what I'm doing and I'm doing it because I want to.' She slipped her jacket off, unzipped her skirt and stepped out of it and her shoes without missing a beat, but her fingers were a little unsteady as she started to unbutton her blouse.

'Why?'

She lifted her eyes to his when she got the last button undone and the blouse slithered off her and fell to the floor. 'I told you, I want to,' she said huskily and took a few steps forward to stand just out of his reach in her bra and half-petticoat. 'I...need to. Do you mind, Liam?'

His lips twisted. 'How could I mind? But——?'

'Then let me do it,' she whispered and pushed the slip down, stepped out of it and reached behind her to release her bra which she took off carefully and folded neatly, staring down at it so that her hair fell forward. Then she dropped it to the floor and raised her head, pushed back her hair and stood before him wearing only a pair of pale grey silk panties, a matching grey lace suspender belt and the sheerest of stockings. And her skin was like ivory satin in the candlelight, her hair like midnight, her breasts small but high and pink-tipped, her eyes nearly as green as her ring as she returned his gaze steadily.

'Jane—come here,' he said at last.

She hesitated a moment then came and he took her hand and drew her to stand between his knees and placed his hands around her waist. 'You didn't have to do that,' he said barely audibly.

'Yes I did. Didn't you like it—or didn't I do it right?' she queried.

'You did it perfectly. I'm not sure I understand *why* though. Unfortunately, the effect it's had on me leaves me in little state to—query it. Do you have any idea how beautiful you are?'

Their eyes locked. 'I'm glad you think so. 'It,' she lifted a hand and touched his hair, 'fills me with joy that you do think——'

She stopped as he took a tortured breath, drew her close and buried his face between her breasts briefly then started to kiss them, his big hands spread over her back and hips. And she tilted her head back and gasped at the sensations he was inflicting on her, the desire that was beginning to course through her like a living tide until she could stand it no longer and her knees gave way and she sank to the carpet and stared up into his eyes... 'Please,' she whispered.

'Jane?'

'Yes, Liam?' she said very softly.

He stirred and cupped her face in his hands staring down into her green eyes. The candles had burnt halfway down. 'How was that?'

She sighed and blinked away a few tears. 'It was—a wondrous experience,' she whispered. 'I don't know how you did it but you made me feel—incredibly sexy and full of all sorts of feelings I didn't know I possessed.' She stopped as she remembered the pure sensuality that had gripped her when they'd lain together on the bed, both naked, both drinking in each other's bodies through their pores, it seemed. Remembered how she'd delighted in the sheer magnificent perfection of his and the delight of offering him her slenderness and softness. How he'd taken all the time in the world to kiss and caress her and guide her down the path of rapture, how her desire had mounted and she'd known he was doing all in his power to make her as ready as possible and save her any hurt.

There'd been a little—a small, sharp tearing sensation that had caused her to catch her breath—but he'd said her name and held her so close as if she was infinitely delicate until it had passed and it had filled her with wonder that such a big, powerful man could be so very gentle . . .

'For a late starter,' she said with a catch in her voice, 'how did I do?'

His fingers moved on her face. 'For a late starter you were inspired.' He smiled but there was something oddly sober in his eyes.

'Why do you look like that?' she whispered, trailing her fingers down his arm.

'How do I look?'

'I—don't know. Rather serious.'

'That might be because I'm afflicted with a serious desire to make love to you again.'

'Oh.' Jane took a breath. 'I wouldn't mind——'

'But I'm not going to.' He ran his fingers through her hair. 'Late starters should take things slowly.'

She moved closer in his arms, filled with love. Then she remembered and she closed her eyes and hid her face against his chest and wondered if she'd have the strength now . . .

'Jane?'

'Yes . . .'

'What's wrong?'

'Nothing—Liam, do late starters have any say in the matter?'

'They—Jane, look at me,' he said slowly.

She did and managed through a sheer effort of will to make her eyes calm. 'Yes?'

'Is there something I don't know about?'

'Yes,' she whispered. 'This.' Her fingers moved. 'I want to say thank you, I want to repay the way you . . . did it. I want to do it to you, with all my heart. But you obviously know a lot more about it than I do so . . . why don't you take my hand and guide it and then I'll know?'

Her breath caught but she steadied it. 'I'll know I'm not making any mistakes, and I'm pleasing you...'

He said something beneath his breath, but she ignored it and twisted free of his arms and got to her knees. And she bent over him so her hair brushed him and she trailed her nipples against his chest and followed their path with her lips, kissing, tasting then she slipped her hand into his and drew it slowly down his body.

He shuddered and this time, when he took her, there were no concessions for late starters, only a man and a woman swept away on a tide of passion.

CHAPTER TEN

PERTH, the capital of Western Australia, was a modern seaside city of some charm, although a lot of that charm was lost on Jane. It was also the last Australian departure port for Quantas flights to Harare, the capital of Zimbabwe and about as far away as Jane could get from Brisbane while she impatiently awaited the completion of all the formalities required for a trip to Africa.

She'd taken a month's unpaid leave from work plus a month of leave overdue to her and she'd done it the day after she'd slept with Liam because she'd known that to delay would place an impossible strain on her resolve that she couldn't marry him.

She'd told no one of her plans. She'd gone to work that morning and simply not returned home that night—she had asked Laura to deliver two notes for her, one to Liam and one to Amanda, on her way home from work, but all Laura and everyone else at work knew was that she was seriously overtired and needed a decent break. Perhaps there'd been enough truth in it for the partner to whom she'd presented her request for extended leave at such awfully short notice to stare at her piercingly and then acquiesce without making too much fuss. And enough pain in her eyes for Laura to start to protest about the wedding then go oddly quiet.

So she'd flown to Perth in what she stood up in, booked herself into a modest motel on the beach, and tried desperately not to feel as if a part of her innermost soul had been torn away.

To help deaden the pain, she'd concentrated on building up a new Jane Mathieson and shedding the old one. A person who, for the first time for years, had time on her hands and a simple lifestyle to live. She bought herself some simple casual clothes and the barest minimum of cosmetics—she was determined to travel light; the heaviest part of her luggage would be the books she bought and these would be a refuge too. And she spent a lot of those days walking, along the beach or taking a bus into town and walking through Kings' Park and along the banks of the Swan River. It was too cold to swim but the crashing surf of the Indian Ocean right outside the motel was somehow soothing.

So it was quite a different image she presented as she trudged along the beach one windy, chilly dusk in a fleecy-lined tracksuit and sand shoes, her mind a couple of thousand miles away on the other side of the continent. Which was why she thought she was hallucinating when she looked up—and in the last of the daylight thought she saw Liam walking towards her.

She stopped dead, waiting for this mirage to disappear, but it didn't. Then she thought she must be mistaken, it was someone who looked like him, had the same build, the same magnificent shoulders, but as he got closer she knew she wasn't—she knew that maroon sweater too well and her first instinct was to turn and run.

She did so, foolishly, then, realising she was being a fool, she turned and yelled at him to go away and leave her alone, but the wind whipped her words away so she started to run again but it was hard work along the beach and she veered towards a dune which was where he caught her. He actually tackled her around the legs but contrived to bring her down gently and precisely and the sand was soft anyway.

All the same she lay panting and helpless as he knelt beside her and after one agitated look into his grimly determined eyes she closed hers and went limp beneath his hands.

'I hesitate to imagine all the fight has gone out of you, Jane, but I can carry you back to the motel or you can walk.'

Her lashes lifted abruptly and all the fight in her came pouring back. 'The last time you did something like this to me it took me *days* to recover,' she said acidly. 'How do you know I can walk?'

'The last time I did something like this to you, you took me by surprise,' he retorted. 'This time I knew exactly what I was doing and I brought you down like a feather.'

Jane sat up. 'That still doesn't give you the right to go around *manhandling* people,' she spat at him. But her voice changed as he moved. 'Liam...no,' she said uncertainly.

'I gave you a choice, Jane,' he said drily, standing up and scooping her into his arms in the one strong movement.

She made a protesting sound but he ignored it and strode down the beach towards the motel.

She tried again. 'I hope there's no one watching this, Liam. You could find yourself trying to explain away a kidnapping charge!'

'As a matter of interest, Jane,' he replied evenly, 'have you ever come across a breach of promise charge in your legal experience?'

'I...' Her tongue seemed to tie itself into knots. 'I... well,' she managed to say finally and went on, 'I'm sure breach of promise works the other way around...' But she trailed off, cursing herself inwardly for making ridiculous statements in the first place and then adding to them.

'Does it, now?' He stopped walking and she saw that they'd arrived at the motel—he set her on to her feet but kept his hands around her waist. 'Talking theoretically, as I'm sure you were doing earlier,' his eyes mocked her, 'what do you imagine an impartial onlooker would make of your actions? You agreed to marry me, you seduced me,' she coloured helplessly as he paused with deadly intent then went on, 'and you left me the very next day with a brief note to the effect that you'd changed your mind,' he finished inexorably.

She bit her lip. 'It's still not—I mean,' she twisted her hands together, 'you weren't... it's not the same!' she said in a rush.

'In some respects not,' he agreed. 'It was your virginity that was lost, although,' he shrugged, 'why you should choose to lose it to a man you didn't ever want to see again would probably be a mystery to the most impartial observer, but we'll deal with that separately— they don't know you as I do,' he said with irony. 'But who's to know what I might have lost? To my knowledge,' he went on deliberately, 'there were no precautions taken by either—party.'

Jane stared up at him, her eyes widening as what he was saying sank in and she gasped then and licked her lips and tried to speak but he overrode her, 'Were there, Jane?'

'No... I mean, no,' she whispered, 'but——'

'Then can you tell me you're not carrying my baby?'

'N-no. I... not yet but I doubt it. I——'

'Well, you could be right but you could be quite wrong——'

'Liam,' she said desperately, 'why are you doing this?'

He took his hands from her waist and smiled but with no amusement. 'You were the one who started talking in legal terms—I sometimes wonder if they're the only terms you understand, but, be that as it may, perhaps we could go inside now and continue this discussion rationally?'

The motel room was small but fairly comfortable with twin beds and in a short space of time Liam had retrieved his bag from Reception, added his name to the register and conjured up some brandy.

Jane sat on one bed—although there were two chairs—during all this and hugged herself dazedly. But finally the door closed for the last time and it was just the two of them and he poured two drinks and put hers into her hand, closing her fingers around the glass as she trembled. But he said nothing and went over to the window with his drink and stood with his back to her, staring over the dark beach.

Jane watched him for a moment then took a gulp of brandy and said unsteadily, 'How did you find me?'

He turned at last. 'Process of elimination. I knew where you would be going; I knew you'd have to pick up a flight in Sydney or Perth.'

'But you must have checked out hundreds of hotels and motels,' she said involuntarily.

'I also knew you were here a few days ago,' he said. 'I have a friend who works for Qantas. He turned up your booking.'

'I might have known,' Jane murmured wearily. 'Liam——' She stopped and sighed and her shoulders sagged. 'I still can't marry you. I know it must seem strange—what I did—but——'

'No stranger than anything else you've done since we got to know each other. Shall I tell you how you did it in case you think I failed to understand? You,' he stopped as she moved restlessly but not for long, 'laid down all your arms, you—went out of your way to make love to me in a particular way that had a unique symbolism for us, that was a complete capitulation, and only a woman deeply in love would have done that. At least that's what I thought at the time. Was I wrong? Did you in fact set out to win what you once termed the "seduction stakes"?'

She winced and wouldn't look at him in case her eyes betrayed her.

'Jane?'

'I—don't want to talk about it.'

'If our positions were reversed wouldn't you think that rather cowardly?' he said with soft but stinging mockery. 'Not even to tell me *why* you changed your mind?'

She breathed deeply. 'Because I knew,' her voice shook, 'that you didn't love me, Liam.'

'Was that before you slept with me or afterwards? Or was it really because I wouldn't let you postpone the wedding? Is that what you based your observation on?'

He smiled dangerously. 'Our impartial onlooker would have a bit of trouble with that, Jane.'

She put a hand to her mouth. 'I—not only that,' she whispered. 'You must know what I mean,' she whispered with a suddenly helpless little gesture.

He stared at her, taking in her pale face and tormented eyes, the unfamiliar casual way she was dressed, the windblown tangle of her hair, the way her fingers were white about the glass as if it was a lifeline she was clinging to—and all of a sudden he appeared to relax. He set his own glass down carefully and came towards the bed but he stopped in front of her and didn't touch her.

'Yes, I know what you mean,' he said after a long moment, 'but things have changed——'

'No...' It was a bare breath of sound but Jane stumbled to her feet agitatedly and spilt her drink. 'I know what you're going to say, I know you're going to try and tell me you do love me but I can't believe you, Liam, you see, and anyway——'

He took the glass from her and grimaced as more brandy was spilt. 'Then I'll have to show you, won't I?' He put the glass down on the bedside table.

'Liam...n-no,' she stammered as he turned back to her. 'You wouldn't...'

He stared down at her then his lips twisted. 'Yes I would, Jane.' And with a spare, precise movement he unzipped the front of her tracksuit.

'I don't...' She trembled visibly. 'I wouldn't have believed this of you, Liam.'

He raised an eyebrow. 'You believe a lot of other things about me.' He took the zip out of its track and slipped the jacket off her shoulders.

She breathed raggedly and clutched her hands in front of her so he couldn't remove it entirely then froze as he looked into her eyes and smiled that lazy, intimate smile that affected her so profoundly.

'Why, Jane,' he murmured, 'you're not wearing a bra.'

She wasn't. Instead she had on a new pale pink singlet with a prim little satin ribbon threaded through the neckline and tied into a bow and the swell of her breasts and the outline of her nipples was clearly visible beneath it.

'I didn't know you wore singlets,' he added, his eyes still laughing at her.

'I don't—usually. I thought...how would you know whether I wore them or not, anyway?' she countered then bit her lip and coloured.

'During the term of our engagement, I spent quite a bit of time with my hands beneath your clothes. I know exactly what you wore. I even knew you'd acquired a taste for frivolous suspender belts and stockings before you—showed me,' he said gravely. 'Tell me something,' his gaze roamed her bare shoulders and the glossy hollows at the base of her throat, 'how does it feel not to be a virgin?'

Her face paled but she set her lips mutinously.

'Lonely? As if a whole new world has opened for you? Or aren't you planning to repeat the experience—you did it so very well,' he said, his lips barely moving but his blue gaze devastating, 'that that would be hard to believe.'

She swallowed convulsively. 'Did you come all this way to insult me, Liam? If so——'

'I didn't, in fact. But I'm interested. Because it must have some bearing on *why* you did it. Like to tell me?'

'I . . . why are you doing this to me?' she whispered, her eyes huge and shadowed.

'Can't there be truth between us, Jane, if nothing else?' He lifted a hand and cupped her shoulder, slipping his fingers beneath the narrow pink strap.

She tried to stay unmoved but it was impossible. Impossible not to be flooded with the memory of lying in his arms feeling silken and softly helpless, completely at his mercy but unafraid because she'd known that no other man could make her feel quite the same and known that she hadn't been strong enough to deny herself the wonder of it, just once. But she'd also known the one thing she could give to Liam Benedict, if she loved him, was his freedom.

'Truth?' she said huskily at last. 'I'm not sure I understand but if you want me to *tell* you I love you, I . . .' She stopped then flinched as his fingers tightened on her shoulder and she took a breath as something hard flared in his eyes.

He also said roughly, 'Yes. I do.'

She stared up at him, her lips parted, her eyes stunned, not sure of anything suddenly because there was something so different about him, so . . . But she couldn't put it into words although she'd seen him angry once before—yet that had been rough and tough but brief and curiously impersonal, which this was not. This was a kind of naked savagery that made her afraid . . .

'I also,' he went on in a clipped curt voice she hardly recognised, 'want to know if you have felt lonely, if you've lain awake at night,' he paused, 'aching for my touch, if your body feels any different to you now—I want to know it all.'

She gasped because there was also a barely concealed crude brutality in it and a flood of anger came to her rescue and her eyes sparked green fire. And she wrenched herself free but stumbled back against the bed and sat down unexpectedly and he caught both her wrists and sat down beside her.

'Tell me, Jane,' he ordered.

'I'm telling you nothing and you can't make me!'

'Yes, I can. Not because I want to but because with you there are times when nothing else works.'

'I *hate* you, Liam,' she said through her teeth and with sudden tears in her eyes and struggled to break free but it was useless. 'All *right*! All of the above and some more, but what good is it going to do either of us——'

'And did you lay down your arms that night and make love to me in honesty and joy—and love?' he shot at her.

She closed her eyes.

'Jane?' he said with soft but unmistakable menace.

Her lashes fluttered up and her eyes were despairing. 'Oh, *yes*,' she said hoarsely, 'but don't you see we're just back to square one where I love you but *you*——?'

'No, *you*,' he said softly, 'have set yourself up as an authority on what I feel. Well, you're wrong, Jane.' He released her wrists abruptly and slipped her tracksuit top back on although he didn't do up the zip. 'The truth of the matter is—I think I fell in love with you not long after you fell through that window.'

'No, you *didn't*—you thought I was the kind of woman who didn't like to go down without a fight and you were *looking* for an affair with a bit of spice, something to liven your life up, you *told* me——'

'I certainly found it,' he said wryly. 'My life hasn't been the same since. But in fact if there was anyone who didn't like to go down without a fight it was me; it was even a point of pride with me.'

She frowned. 'You were the one who...'

'Wanted to sleep with you?' he supplied. 'Oh, yes. I was also the one who thought to begin with that I could end it with no hard feelings and walk out of your life when I chose. You have to admit I was quite wrong there.' He raised a quizzical eyebrow at her and grimaced.

She licked her lips. 'But——'

'Jane,' he put his hand over hers, clutched together tensely again and all of a sudden his eyes were completely serious, even bleakly so, 'if you're not there the very air I breathe is lacking something despite everything I may have intimated to the contrary——'

He broke off, as she moved urgently, then said, 'Listen, just listen to me, Jane... At least let me tell you why I was the way I was.' He stopped and a nerve flickered in his jaw then he raised his blue eyes to hers and they were sombre as he said evenly, 'I got trapped once. By a girl who for all that she mightn't have been—my soul-mate, was also very young and——' He stopped and gestured. 'Yes, I *have* always felt guilty as hell about Maureen and Rory—you were right about that. And it has always been a problem to sort the...' He grimaced.

'Wheat from the chaff,' Jane said involuntarily.

He smiled a little drily. 'Not that so much, but I've spent a lot of years trying to protect myself, as I saw it, from creating that kind of misery again.'

'It mightn't have helped being the kind of man who looks like the answer to every woman's prayer,' she said ruefully, but added with spirit, 'I don't know why you won't admit it!'

'Now, Jane, you yourself told me it was—wicked? I think that's the word you used, to trade on anything like that,' he pointed out wryly.

'I was wrong—I mean you don't,' she said gloomily then licked her lips uncertainly.

'Well, be that as it may,' he sobered, 'until I met you, I was quite happy the way I was. Then I became—at first it was like a kind of disorientation. I knew, I always knew I had to have you, I just refused to believe it couldn't be on *my* terms, but there was something else sort of lurking over my shoulder. I now realise it was the growing knowledge that you were the one girl I didn't want to hurt but that wanting you and still being afraid to trust myself in a no-holds-barred relationship—was the one sure way of hurting you terribly.'

She stared at him, breathing raggedly, several different expressions chasing through her eyes and the tiny seed of hope in her heart that she was at last getting through to the real Liam Benedict.

'So I regrouped as best I could,' he went on rather grimly. 'I told myself it wasn't too late, you weren't sure of your feelings, you were confused and traumatised and I'd never forgive myself for adding to it. And I tried to explain how things were for me.' He paused. 'What I neglected to explain was that—it was already too late for me.'

She made a husky little sound and he took her face in his hands. 'Then, things happened the way they happened and I knew I couldn't live without you, that I'd been fooling myself to imagine I could ever walk away from you—even on two good legs. I still had to have you, Jane, in other words,' he said very quietly. 'But I thought, in my lingering cynicism, that I would be able to get away with putting it all down to a sane, rational decision. That I would be better not laying too much of myself on the line because that way I could stay in some sort of control. I was wrong.' He stared down into her eyes with so much self-directed irony that she caught her breath.

'So—if you really want to know why I wouldn't let you postpone the wedding,' he went on, 'it was not because I didn't understand how much it would mean to you to have your father present but because I was afraid he'd prevail on you to change your mind. And deadly afraid after you left that you'd come to the conclusion that all those things I once tried to tell you were true. That you were lonely, that your hormones were finally winning through and that—you'd decided to experiment with me...'

She stilled incredulously. 'You... thought that?'

'I thought all sorts of things.' He stared into her eyes and she trembled suddenly. 'Can I tell you what I'm thinking now?' he added. 'That I'm longing to take off your pretty pink singlet to see if there's a single sign that you might be pregnant, and if that's not an indication of a man deeply, irretrievably, proudly, *sentimentally* and hopelessly in love I don't know what is—I do know if anyone had told me I'd ever feel this way I might not have believed them but there you go...' He stopped and smiled but with an effort. 'I've also bought myself a ticket to Harare. I thought, with your approval, we could take the wedding to him.'

'Liam...' Jane swallowed several times and discovered there were new tears slipping down her cheeks and he put his hand over hers. 'But you were angry with me, you were...' She stopped helplessly.

'Angry,' he agreed drily, 'but because I was desperate for reassurance.'

Her eyes widened. 'You...were?' she whispered. 'I mean, I've never seen you like that before.'

He grimaced. 'I've never felt like that before.'

The silence lengthened as she stared at him with a kind of wonder dawning in her eyes.

Then he moved as if to take her into his arms but restrained himself. 'Don't look like that,' he said very quietly. 'I've been an incredible fool all along and I've done nothing but browbeat you and *manhandle* you since I got here. But the fact is all those things I was so bloody sanctimonious about when I proposed to you had already happened to me and I'll probably spend the rest of our lives being——' his lips twisted '—being quite irrational where you're concerned.'

'So long as you're also in love with me, I don't think I'll mind.'

'You—just now you said you hated me.'

Jane considered, then said gravely, 'Well, yes, I think we ought to take that into consideration too. I sometimes do and say crazy things. That was one of them. But,' she stopped and smiled up at him, a trembling little smile close to tears again, 'the truth is, the hardest thing I ever did in my life was leave you. I felt—I've felt, oh, Liam,' her voice broke, 'I love you. Please hold me or something. Tell me this is real and not some...'

He said her name on a harsh breath and gathered her into his arms as if he'd never let her go.

* * *

It was very early the next morning that she said to him, 'Can you detect any signs of—that we might be parents-to-be?'

A slightly wicked glint disturbed the lazy blue of his eyes. 'Sit up and I'll have a good look.'

She sat up on her heels then hesitated and drew a sudden breath as he crossed his arms behind his head and that lazy gaze roamed her body.

'Liam——'

'Mmm?'

'This—wasn't quite what I had in mind.'

'Why not?' He withdrew one hand, touched one nipple then the other with a featherlight touch and let his hand slide down to her waist and the soft curve of her stomach.

'Well—I was serious.'

'So am I,' he murmured, but his eyes were laughing at her and as she looked down at him, at the blue shadows on his jaw, the way his hair lay on his forehead, she was suffused with a helpless longing to slip back into his arms, but, being Jane, admonished herself rather sternly. I mean, I can't spend my whole life in his arms, can I? she told herself.

'And it's a serious matter, anyway, isn't it?' she added, trying to sound serious but sounding quite prim instead—to her annoyance.

'Oh, it is,' he agreed. 'The subject of a lifelong pre-occupation, I suspect. Do you know what you remind me of?' he went on as she opened her mouth. 'An exquisite figurine. All ivory and rose and so delicate I'm afraid sometimes——' He grimaced.

Her eyes widened. 'Why?'

'That I'll hurt you.'

'You never have. But I used to worry about that too,' she confessed.

'Did you, now?' His lips twitched. 'Was that when you were insulting me or—just throwing things at me?'

Jane blushed. 'No, I mean I used to wonder what it would be like—I mean I thought this would have to be a very vulnerable experience but it's...just lovely.'

He smiled a little wryly and drew her down into his arms. 'Thanks for those kind words, lady.'

'Is it—the same for you?' she queried.

'Well, despite your belief that I had a predilection for buxom, Amazonian women, it's unlike anything that's ever happened to me. It also keeps happening to me, especially when you do that.'

Jane removed her hand. 'You didn't tell me,' she murmured.

'Whether there were any signs? No, there aren't, but that could be because it's still too soon.'

She was silent and he said presently, 'What are you thinking?'

'That only a few hours ago I was feeling devastated and now—this,' she said a bit shakily. 'I'm sorry, I really didn't think I was the kind of woman who could have a good cry but——'

'If Sam were here he'd tell me I should be shot—he's right,' Liam said drily. 'Are you still having doubts?'

'No, but I'm thinking,' she drew a quivering breath but managed to smile through her tears, 'that I was a much tougher nut when I was a virgin and that I could be a great trial to you now in a different way. I've also become a...toucher and a cuddler beyond my wildest expectations, so you see——'

'Jane.' He ran his fingers through her hair and cupped her face and kissed her lingeringly then he said, not quite smiling, 'Whether you're chastising me on the error of my ways or spitting at me like an outraged kitten as I'm sure you'll do from time to time despite becoming such an expert toucher and cuddler—I *love* you. I always will.'

**Fifty red-blooded, white-hot, true-blue hunks
from every State in the Union!**

Look for MEN MADE IN AMERICA! Written by some of our most poplar authors, these stories feature fifty of the strongest, sexiest men, each from a different state in the union!

Two titles available every other month at your favorite retail outlet.

In March, look for:

TANGLED LIES by Anne Stuart (Hawaii)
ROGUE'S VALLEY by Kathleen Creighton (Idaho)

In May, look for:

LOVE BY PROXY by Diana Palmer (Illinois)
POSSIBLES by Lass Small (Indiana)

You won't be able to resist MEN MADE IN AMERICA!

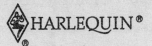

HARLEQUIN®

COMING SOON TO
A STORE NEAR YOU...

THE MAIN
ATTRACTION

By *New York Times* Bestselling Author

This March, look for THE MAIN ATTRACTION by popular
author Jayne Ann Krentz.

Ten years ago, Filomena Cromwell had left her small town
in shame. Now she is back determined to get her sweet,
sweet revenge....

Soon she has her ex-fiancé, who cheated on her with
another woman, chasing her all over town. And he isn't
the only one. Filomena lets Trent Ravinder catch her.

Can she control the fireworks she's set into motion?

HARLEQUIN®

Don't miss these Harlequin favorites by some of our most distinguished authors!
And now, you can receive a discount by ordering two or more titles!

HT#25409	THE NIGHT IN SHINING ARMOR by JoAnn Ross	$2.99 ☐
HT#25471	LOVESTORM by JoAnn Ross	$2.99 ☐
HP#11463	THE WEDDING by Emma Darcy	$2.89 ☐
HP#11592	THE LAST GRAND PASSION by Emma Darcy	$2.99 ☐
HR#03188	DOUBLY DELICIOUS by Emma Goldrick	$2.89 ☐
HR#03248	SAFE IN MY HEART by Leigh Michaels	$2.89 ☐
HS#70464	CHILDREN OF THE HEART by Sally Garrett	$3.25 ☐
HS#70524	STRING OF MIRACLES by Sally Garrett	$3.39 ☐
HS#70500	THE SILENCE OF MIDNIGHT by Karen Young	$3.39 ☐
HI#22178	SCHOOL FOR SPIES by Vickie York	$2.79 ☐
HI#22212	DANGEROUS VINTAGE by Laura Pender	$2.89 ☐
HI#22219	TORCH JOB by Patricia Rosemoor	$2.89 ☐
HAR#16459	MACKENZIE'S BABY by Anne McAllister	$3.39 ☐
HAR#16466	A COWBOY FOR CHRISTMAS by Anne McAllister	$3.39 ☐
HAR#16462	THE PIRATE AND HIS LADY by Margaret St. George	$3.39 ☐
HAR#16477	THE LAST REAL MAN by Rebecca Flanders	$3.39 ☐
HH#28704	A CORNER OF HEAVEN by Theresa Michaels	$3.99 ☐
HH#28707	LIGHT ON THE MOUNTAIN by Maura Seger	$3.99 ☐

Harlequin Promotional Titles

#83247	YESTERDAY COMES TOMORROW by Rebecca Flanders	$4.99 ☐
#83257	MY VALENTINE 1993	$4.99 ☐
	(short-story collection featuring Anne Stuart, Judith Arnold, Anne McAllister, Linda Randall Wisdom)	

(limited quantities available on certain titles)

	AMOUNT	$
DEDUCT:	10% DISCOUNT FOR 2+ BOOKS	$
ADD:	POSTAGE & HANDLING	$
	($1.00 for one book, 50¢ for each additional)	
	APPLICABLE TAXES*	$ _____
	TOTAL PAYABLE	$ _____
	(check or money order—please do not send cash)	

To order, complete this form and send it, along with a check or money order for the total above, payable to Harlequin Books, to: **In the U.S.:** 3010 Walden Avenue, P.O. Box 9047, Buffalo, NY 14269-9047; **In Canada:** P.O. Box 613, Fort Erie, Ontario, L2A 5X3.

Name: _____

Address: _____ City: _____

State/Prov.: _____ Zip/Postal Code: _____

*New York residents remit applicable sales taxes.
 Canadian residents remit applicable GST and provincial taxes.

HBACK-JM